STEAMY DREAMS 2

Kali's Revenge

Ms. T. Lane

Moore's Publishing House

Moore's Publishing
Certified Publisher

ISBN (eBook): 979-8-9985250-5-6

ISBN (Paperback): 979-8-9985250-6-3

Cover design by **Nubian FX**

Printed in the United States of America

This is a work of fiction. Names, characters, places, and incidents are either the product of the author's imagination or used fictitiously. Any resemblance to actual persons, living or dead, or real events is purely coincidental.

Published by Moore's Publishing House

2

Dedication

I dedicate this book to:

My Mother Teni D. Moore, who taught me to never give up on my dreams and to fight for what is right. R.I.P Mommy I love you and I miss you very much. And my Grandparents Geri and LeeVada who raised me with stability and a strong moral standing.

Thank You for everything. I love you all.

Acknowledgements

I'd like to thank all my family and friends who supported my book from the beginning. All of those that encouraged me to never stop writing. Those that read all the rough drafts, the re-reads and the finales.

I'd like to thank a very good childhood friend, Michelle Givens, who read and paid cash for my first book, and demanded part two the moment she finished the first one.

Mary Ann Joseph who gave me my first official book sale.

I'd like to thank God for never giving up on me, even when I was lost in darkness, he continued to hold my hand, protect me and guide me. Even when I had given up on him he never gave up on me. Thank You Father. I am truly humbled.

Kischa McKnight for giving me her very own copies of books to read that inspired Steamy Dreams.

B.I.G Malo for reminding me, "what God got for me can't no- body take from me."

I would like to give an extra special thanks to Unika Oliver, a great friend and manager who had the guts to promote me even though I was seven months pregnant and continued to support me throughout my writing career. I appreciate you so much for believing in me. Thanks Nikki and may God Bless You!

There may be a few names that I may have forgotten to men- tion and if I did forgive me, but please know by looking at me, reading my work and supporting me, you will shine through me.

And to my readers that have paid their hard-earned green dollars supporting ya girl, I didn't forget about you. My love for each and every one of you kindles my heart each time you purchase, download or even share my work with others. I literally thrive on knowing that someone out there is not only reading my work but enjoys it and loves it just as much as I enjoy writing it, if not more. I give a big "Niecy" hug to every single one of you.

God Bless and as always,

Make today Greater than yesterday! ~Ms. T.

Preface

I've been writing since the age of sixteen. My mother always told me I had a way with words. I remember a time when she caught me on the phone having a less than pleasant conversation with a boy I was dating, and her reaction was unbelievable. I just knew I was about to get ripped a new one, but it was just the opposite. Her exact words were "Damn girl you put together curse words better than I do."

I was embarrassed and proud all at the same time. I guess you could say my mom had a bit of a potty mouth, but it was never vulgar. I once read that people who use foul language tend to be the most honest and that was my mother "Honest T." Maybe that was her downfall, because she wore her heart on her sleeve. The great relationship and bond my mother and I had developed would be short lived. In 1998 I found out that my mother was addicted to a drug commonly known in my neighborhood as crack cocaine. Being left to raise myself and my little brother I leaned on my writing to get me through the emotional upset. I would write everywhere. Restaurant napkins, bills, walls, any blank slate would become my canvas.

The one thing I noticed that was different about my writing from many others, was the role passion played in most of my material. I enjoyed writing about sexual encounters that I hadn't even experienced yet. This is very difficult to explain to the world when you're a child. I buried that side of me for a long time, but it would soon erupt when I became dissatisfied in my marriage. By the time I turned 30 I was pregnant with my second child and my marriage was beginning to disintegrate.

The passion was gone and we both were considerably unsatisfied with each other. Infidelity had become a routine on my husband's part and mentally I had checked out. This was when Steamy Dreams was born. I began to live out my very own fantasies through the characters I created. I was transforming from just a writer to an urban romance author and it was happening rather quickly.

Today I am a divorcee, and it is my hope that Kali, Shonte', MC Brooklyn and Ronny will help others learn to let go of their problems and enjoy their fantasies the same way I did. My dream is to have Steamy Dreams in every household, library, book store and even adult novelty places, so everyone can get the enjoyment of being seduced by the love tones of the Steamy Dreams Series.

Speaking of Miss Kali, I introduce her in Steamy Dreams II as a thrill seeking, obsessed, luxury driven, knock-out- gorgeous, sexy seductress that has a secret that may bring MC Brooklyn's entire operation down to its knees.

Shonte' and MC Brooklyn return to this romantic love story with even more drama and passion than before. Shonte's life has changed quite a bit, but sex, lies, money and steamy secrets always find their way back to her. The psychic intuition grows deeper and clearer in her dreams and its running in overdrive. Shonte' is on the clock to make sure things don't turn out like in her not so steamy dream.

No matter how hard she tries to get Brooklyn to cooperate, he has plans of his own. Shonte' has caused him great sadness and grief, and he has no plans of forgiving her any time soon. His feelings of Anger, disgust and resentment get the best of him, which will lead him right into the arms of label mate "Killa Kali." He can't get her out of his mind and right now he doesn't really want to, they have a connection that goes far beyond the glitzy and glamorous stage lights.

Will Shonte' and Brooklyn figure out what Kali's secret is before it's too late? Or will Kali end up fending for her life, trying to escape the fears of a powerful woman having steamy dreams?

This Steamy Romance Sequel will leave you craving passion even more than the first one. Steamy Dreams part 1 is one of the most unique stories for adults you will ever read, and there's much more where that came from.

Stay Tuned!

Until Next Time Steamy Dreamers…

Ms. T. Lane

Introduction

If you didn't read Steamy Dreams Part 1, where have you been? Steamy Dreams Part I introduces the main character Shonte' with a bang. It starts off fueled with sensual desires that Shonte's husband Michael cannot fulfill. She finds herself prophesying her very own fantasies. Although she knows what's going to happen before it does, that doesn't stop her from making quite a few questionable decisions.

Shonte' finds herself in a whirlwind of trouble when she seemingly gets involved with a local rapper and football player, against her husband's wishes. The obsession of one of her lovers leads to murder, attempted murder, sexual informalities, investigations and a slew of other events.

Steamy Dreams II, reintroduces Shonte's sexual desires, however the dreams have taken a back seat. Shonte' finds herself happy and sexually satisfied with a previous lover, which causes a numbing effect to her ability to prophesize. Although Shonte's happiness is a good thing, losing her ability to see future events may not be so great.

In this sequel Shonte', Michael, MC Brooklyn, Ronny and Kali all find themselves trying to break free of the dominant hold of Shonte' and her prophecies. But she won't allow it.

There is more drama, luxury, sensual moments, excitement, danger, police investigations, secrets, infidelity, high powered romance, lies and deceit than its predecessor, Steamy Dreams Part 1. This time Shonte' and the new girl Kali go head up. The question is: who will lose?

~Ms. T.

Chapter 1: Brooklyn and Shonte'

Shonte' was finally happy with Brooklyn. They managed to have the perfect life together. A beautiful eight-bedroom mansion with many amenities like sub zero refrigerators and a bidet in every bathroom. Chandeliers fell from the ceiling like rain, the walls were the purest of white. They had a giant four-car garage with brand-name cars like Bugatti, Maserati, and Maybach, plus a jet on the runway at the airport. Needless to say, Shonte' could wake up every day in a new Bugatti. Her life was the best it had ever been. She walked around their mansion as if she couldn't believe it was her reality. Her bare- naked feet against the cold marble floors only reminded her that it was definitely real.

As she entered their master bedroom she plopped down on the Egyptian cotton bedspread with black and gold décor, and thought to herself, *now this is what happiness really feels like.*

Shonte' began to think about her life with Brooklyn. *I wonder if he's going to change now that he's a mega star? I hope he doesn't become a snob*, she thought to herself. "Nah... I doubt it, he's way too Brooklyn," she said with a devilish smile. It would be awesome if we could be like those celebrity couples you see on T.V.

Then a thought struck her mind like a flash of lightning. *I wonder how he would feel if I proposed to him in our favorite place to visit, Dubai.* Shonte' knew this idea was risky but if anyone could pull it off she sure could. Yes. That's it, I'm going to do it! I will plan for it and surprise him for his birthday!

The first time Shonte' and Brooklyn visited Dubai, the trip was short and sweet, due to the time restraints with Brooklyn's tour. Brooklyn promised Shonte' that when time was allotted he would be sure to get her back there someday real soon.

*

M.C. Brooklyn and his entourage entered the building on Park Avenue in New York City to do a radio interview. They mobbed passed the front desk and made a beeline straight for the elevators.

During the ride up, Brooklyn began to think about how wonderful his life has turned out.

Each time a bell rang announcing the next floor it brought him back to reality. However, he was briefly able to lose himself and his thoughts drifted from his travels with Shonte', to wondering if he could spend the rest of his life with her. He even said out loud to one of his comrades, "Man, I've almost lost my life a few times and Shon- te has been there for me. I think I love this one bro. I just might have to marry…."

"BING! 14th Floor," the robotic voice announced. Brooklyn and his entourage exited the elevator.

"What is it you were saying homie?" one of his comrades asked.

"Nothing never-mind bro. Let's just get this work done today." Brooklyn was dressed in his red and black bomber jacket with an Africa symbol on the back, dark blue jeans and oversized black hoodie. Brooklyn smiled in amazement when looking around the studio at the posters of himself as he strolled down the long hallway of the radio station.

"Dope track Brooklyn, can't wait for the album," a young man said passing by.

"Good lookin out bro and album coming real soon!" Brooklyn started to rock his head as his single began to play when he entered the studio.

"Yo Brooklyn, my main man, whaddup homie? You're right on time." The radio announcer greeted Brooklyn with a smile and a brotherly hug.

"Well you know, God is good all the time," he replied.

"Have a seat, put on these headphones and if you're ready we are on in 1-2-3... Hey we are back and joining us live straight outta Brooklyn, it is the man himself M.C. Brooklyn. Thanks for coming down today and if you don't mind can we ask you a few questions?" "Sure, go right ahead," Brooklyn replied.

"So, Brooklyn, what advice would you offer to the young kids still in the game?"

Brooklyn was daydreaming about Shonte'. Thoughts drifted in and out of his mind about how his new life would be if he married Shonte'. He didn't respond to the radio show host, there was silence.

"Brooklyn… Man, you alright over there."

"Yeah man, my bad I was thinking, but to answer your question this is my advice. I can't tell people what to do, but I can tell you and show you what *not* to do. My life wasn't easy and neither is anyone's, but I can guarantee you this, you get out of life exactly what you put into it. So, if you want to sell dope, that's your life, but please understand this, with that same choice you are also choosing your consequences. Don't be mad when those consequences show you exactly what your choices were."

"Spoken like a true soldier that has definitely lived a real life. Ok. You know I gotta ask you this one. Your fans would be mad if I didn't ask you this one right here. Are you single, married, dating an- yone special right now?"

"Ah man. Why you wanna put me on the spot like that? Aint some of these questions off limits?"

"Hey you ain't gotta answer, but your fans would like to know."

"Let's just say I am officially single but if a good woman comes along and snatches me up, then I guess it's *Game Over* for Brooklyn." The entire room laughed with Brooklyn.

"Ok, last question. When you get ready to record, is there anything special you do to get your mind ready. I mean how do you come up with these dope-ass lyrics?"

"Funny thing is, I really don't know. It's like once I hear a beat the words just come to me. Most people hear a sound when they hear a beat, but when I hear a beat it sounds like the soothing voice of a mature woman speaking to me. If you can make sense of that then I guess that answers your question on how I come up with this shit."

"Wow, you never cease to amaze me Brooklyn. All I can say is wow. Well thank you, Brooklyn. We know you're a busy man and you stopped in briefly so we don't want to hold you up. We appreciate your time in doing this interview for us. We need more people like you man. Keep it up."

"No, I appreciate you guys for allowing me to do this. And to show my appreciation to my fans, who always support me in everything I do, I will be giving away ten front row tickets with V.I.P passes to my upcoming concert to the first ten callers that can name my last two albums."

"There you have it folks, the one and only M.C. Brooklyn is always delivering a positive message, and he's always giving back. And on that note, here's his latest hit rightly titled 'Game Over'. You heard it first on the station that plays only platinum hits 99.6 F.M. You know!"

The radio announcer played Brooklyn's song as he exited the building. He couldn't help but feel proud and amazed at the same time. He shook his head in disbelief.

The melody had a sweet sound of an R&B track, with the baseline of the most hardcore rap song that ever existed. It had people grooving on the dance floor and nodding their heads in their cars. Needless to say, the track was banging.

Brooklyn's single Game Over had become a number one hit. It talked about his time on the streets as a dope dealer, how he gracefully bowed out and turned his life around. Game Over literally changed the hip-hop game. It inspired other artists to leave the dope game and join him on the road to inspiring others in his community.

"Who would have ever thought I would be here right now. A little boy from the Brooklyn projects topping the billboard charts," he said to himself and continued on through the glass doors of the building.

Brooklyn was still humming the song and bobbing his head as he exited the building and got into his Bugatti that was parked right in front of the building, awaiting his arrival.

The Bugatti roared louder than usual as Brooklyn stepped on the gas and merged onto the highway. There was something about the open road ahead of him that gave him exhilaration, ambition and a reason to keep making great music. He wasn't sure if it was the sound of the Bugatti or the smell of the burnt rubber when he skirted out of the plaza at the radio station. Whichever it was, his adrenaline was on an all-time high.

"Yeah! I fucking love this shit!" he shouted as he picked up speed. While coasting and enjoying his moment of freedom on the open road, he remembered a meeting he had scheduled with Michael.

Michael was still Brooklyn's agent and managed his career. He used Brooklyn's fake death to advance him to superstardom.

Brooklyn decided to give Michael a call to confirm their meeting for today at his mansion.

"Call Michael."

"Calling Michael," Siri repeated.

"Aye bro, we still good to meet up today at my place?"

"Yes Brooklyn, I will be there shortly."

"Aight, see you then."

Brooklyn turned up the music as loud as it could go. His favorite artist was Tupac Shakur whom he gives a lot of credit to for inspiring him. The song that blared loudly was called "Young Niggaz". It reminded him of the years he spent on the streets. The more he enjoyed the song the faster the car went; he rolled the windows down and allowed the cold New York breeze to flow through the car like it was sweeping him away.

Brooklyn was racing on the highway in and out of traffic. Before he realized it, he was up to one-thirty mph and noticed that he had just passed a police officer who was parked on the side of the freeway. The police car shook as Brooklyn blew by. Immediately the officer turned on the flashing lights and attempted to pull him over.

Brooklyn looked in the rear-view mirror and noticed the police car behind him. As he looked at the flashing lights in his rear view he also looked at himself and said out loud, "You can out run them, nigga. You're in a Bugatti." Brooklyn took his own advice and stepped on it. The police car and flashing lights were getting smaller and smaller until they were gone from his view.

"Y'all can't see me...You can't catch a muthafuckin Bugatti," Brooklyn yelled with fire in his voice. "This ain't the first time I got away from the police and it won't be the last. Fuck the police. Fuckers can't catch me. Brooklyn zoomed as fast as the car could go until he was sure he had lost them.

Shit now I gotta park this muthfucka. This shits probably going to be on the news, then the choppers gonna be after me. I gotta ditch this bitch. Quick!"

"Call Chelly."

"Calling Chelly," Siri replied.

"Hello", the succulent voice said on the other end.

"Babe... are you busy?"

"No Brooklyn, why do you ask? Are you finna come and give me some of that D?"

"Not today baby, I got a bigger job for you. I need to ditch the whip for a few days."

"Oh," she said in a disappointing voice. "How long this time Brook?"

"I don't know for a few months or so… I might have to start a fire. I can't say too much on this phone, but you know what I'm talking about right? Can you handle that for me?"

"Yes Brooklyn, I got you."

Chelly and Brooklyn hadn't messed around in years but no matter how, what, when or where – she always did exactly as he asked.

Brooklyn pulled up to Chelly's quaint home in the South Bronx. "Damn Brooklyn, a Bugatti?" She asked. "How the hell am I supposed to get rid of this?"

Brooklyn got out and gave her a hug and a nice pat on her bottom. "You know what to do baby", he said with a smirk. Brooklyn pulled out a wad of cash. "Is this enough?"

"Brooklyn, I'm gonna need about five racks for this one."

He obliged. "We good," he asked.

"Of course, we are." She leaned in to give Brooklyn a kiss, he backed away. "What's wrong, don't you miss me," she asked.

"Of course, I miss you girl, but by the looks of that ring on your finger you not missing me."

"Whatever Brooklyn I don't even wanna hear it. I will let you know when the job is finished."

Brooklyn pulled the Bugatti into her garage. "So, what you got for me to dip out in? Can I get the Audi A6?"

"Damnit Brooklyn, I just got that car." But Chelly could never say no to Brooklyn. "The key is under the mat, just hit the button and it's yours." She sighed through gritted teeth.

"Thank you baby," he said and winked his eye at her.

Brooklyn hopped in the car, blew Chelly a kiss, slowly backed out the driveway and coasted down the highway. He even passed by a few officers on the way home.

Brooklyn tried to remain inconspicuous by removing his NY hat and putting on his glasses with the clear lenses. He called this his square guy disguise. The only way for Brooklyn to get home was to pass directly through a police barrier. "Fuck! I hope this works."

His heart was beating rapidly and his body was letting off heat. He took a deep breath as his vehicle approached the officer's and their roadblock.

Brooklyn rolled the window down. "Hello, hi there officers. What's going on?"

"Some lunatic in a Bugatti is tearing the goddamn highway to shreds. Have you seen anything?" The officer flashed his light inside the vehicle and overlooked the black NY hat lying in the passenger seat.

"No sir, I haven't seen anything like that at all. He should be arrested." Brooklyn said properly.

"Ok sir, you can go ahead." The officer waved him through.

"Thank You, Mr. officer, and I really hope you guys catch that creep."

"Shit that was close," he exclaimed.

Brooklyn coasted at forty-five mph and continued on his journey to meet with Michael at his posh mansion.

Shonte' was sprawled across the king sized bed in their master bedroom relaxing in her favorite Victoria's secret sweatpants and matching shirt that read pink across her round bottom. "Coming," Shonte' said. She had been interrupted from reading about the latest Kardashian news on her cell phone by the doorbell. She jogged down the gallery style stairs and opened the large wooden double doors. Shonte' gasped as soon as the doors parted. Her jaw dropped and her eyes were at the top of her eyelids.

"Surprised to see me?" the man asked. "Close your mouth, you'll let flies in. Wait, that's right, you like that sort of thing don't you?"

"Michael? What are you doing here? Last time I saw you, you were running out of that hotel room with your tail tucked." Shonte' gave him a devious smile.

Michael was dressed in his Sunday best. Gray suit, pink tie and handkerchief, and a pair of loafers that would make even the richest man in the world envious. He smelled and looked like he could be a spokesperson for Calvin Klein. "Nice to see you too Ms. Smith. Or is it Mrs. Smith? Wait don't answer that, I can see by your bare knuckle that there hasn't been any type of commitment." He smiled with his eyes. "So, are you going to let me in or are we just gonna stand here and continue to banter for the rest of the day?"

Shonte' stepped to the side. As Michael passed her, he softly said, "You seem to be taking that news about the baby pretty lightly, and from what I can see, you are still living off of me." He glanced around their million-dollar mansion, with his nose turned up and said, "I told you that you were nothing without me."

"What are you talking about? What baby?" Shonte' asked. She chose to ignore his sarcastic comments. After all, he was a past lover and she understood the rude gestures were only stemming from his inability to please her in the bedroom. She was taught to have mercy on a man when it is realized he has reached his weakest point, and she knew Michael had reached his.

"Oh," Michael gasped. "You didn't know? I'm sorry. Maybe you should check your Twitter feed."

"Michael my man!" Brooklyn walked in and startled them both. "What's up bro?" Brooklyn went to give Michael an urban hand shake and Michael just stood there stiff bodied as if he had never had a black man hug him in such a way.

"Aw come on Poindexter, you don't even know the hood handshake?" Brooklyn put his hands on his sides and shook his head in disappointment. He glanced over at Shonte'. "What's wrong? You look upset. You ok?"

Shonte' looked at Michael. "Nothing," she mumbled beneath her breath. She turned and walked into the kitchen.

Brooklyn eyed Michael. "What happened to her? What did you say to her?"

"I didn't say anything." Michael was avoiding eye contact with Brooklyn.

"You lying muthafucka." Brooklyn stepped closer to Michael. So close that Michael could feel his breath as Brooklyn softly spoke to him. "Look, Imma tell you like this. Don't ever think that because you were successful with that fake death spin on my career that I still won't fuck you up." Brooklyn slammed the liquor glass on the table and began to pour himself a drink.

"I hear you Brooklyn, but you and I both know we need each other. From the first day right there in my office we knew that we were good for each other. With my great business sense and your talent, we are going to continue to make each other rich for life. Also know this, I never allow personal shit to interfere with my business and I hope you feel the same way."

"That shit is business and Shonte', well she is personal. If I find out you ever did anything, so much as letting a drop of rain land on her head, we got a problem. I mean, if y'all are in the same room together, she shouldn't have to lift a finger, not even to change the channel. You work for me so that means you work for her too. You got that, Poindexter?"

"Yeah Brooklyn I got it, now can we get down to business?"

"Of course, we can. Glad we could come to an understanding."

They both sat down on the cream-colored Italian leather couch. Michael sat his briefcase on the glass table, opened it up and began discussing their new contract.

Shonte' was peeking through the kitchen door, and was getting turned on by the way Brooklyn stood up for her. "No one has ever done that for me before," she whispered to herself. The smile on her face reached from ear to ear, her body became relaxed and her chest was warm with joy.

Her phone started to buzz and it immediately took her away from her gazing. It was a text from her friend Monique.

"Tay, don't believe that shit, them bitches just want your man, call me if you need to talk".

Shonte' replied with three question marks. Monique was taking too long to respond. Shonte' needed to know what was going on. She quickly signed in to her Twitter page to see what all this fuss was about. The trending topic jumped out at her instantly.

MC Brooklyn's gonna be a dad.

There were so many comments. One after another, insult after insult. Shonte' started to feel like she was being personally attacked and for absolutely nothing. She had not done anything and yet these people were upset with her for some strange reason. Shonte' felt herself getting infuriated but she continued to read anyway.

The tweets got worse as she read on and Shonte' began to feel some type of way. One tweet called her stupid for being with him, and others just flat out degraded her as a human being.

A sharp burning pain entered her chest and she became breathless. Shonte' began to hyperventilate. The more she tried to catch her breath the more breath she lost. She tried to catch her balance by holding on to the table, but instead knocked all of the Mikasa dishes on the floor and finally passed out.

While unconscious, Shonte' could vaguely hear Brooklyn's voice as he said, "Man, I'm looking forward to another two years. I appreciate you."

Brooklyn shut the wooden doors of their posh home, but he still felt something wasn't quite right with Michael. He stood at the door and watched Michael drive off through the glass on the wooden door. I don't trust this dude at all, he thought. He placed a phone call to one of his body guards that was standing at the golden gate of his mansion. "Dre, do me a favor and follow this car that's leaving right now. Let me know his every move. You got me?"

"I got you boss," the voice replied.

Brooklyn hung up the phone. "Shonte'," he exclaimed. "Shonte' baby, where are you?" he said in a singing voice.

As Brooklyn entered the kitchen, he saw Shonte' lying passed out on the floor, her body was laid out like a Jesus cross. "Shonte'," he yelled nervously. "Why is all this glass on the floor?" Brooklyn was in disbelief and stunned momentarily. He almost didn't know what to do.

"Oh Shit! What the…" He shook her and felt for a pulse. Once he realized she was still breathing, he stepped away to grab a cold towel, and began rubbing it over her face and body. "Baby wake up. What's wrong with you girl? Wake up." Shonte' snapped out of it with a deep gasp. "Damn! I thought I lost you for a minute."

Shonte' looked up at him, still gasping for breath. "No… No… No… Get away from me Brooklyn." Shonte's eyes welled with tears. Her chest was burning with pain. Her sniffles became critical and she was so choked up she wasn't even able to speak clearly anymore. Her words became a blurred mess and then she got down right angry. She picked up a piece of the broken glass and threw it at Brooklyn. He ducked, she picked up another piece and launched it in his direction.

"Shonte', have you lost your fucking mind?" Brooklyn exclaimed.

The more he spoke the more hostile she became. The last piece she threw at him caught Brooklyn as he was walking towards her and cut his arm. Brooklyn checked the injury on his right forearm and there was a slight cut above the tattoo that read, 'never trust a bitch.'

"Girl what the fuck is wrong with you? Look at what you did. You see this shit. Now I'm bleeding. Girl you better be glad I fucking love yo ass." He grabbed a dish towel from the drawer and began nursing his wound. "What the fuck Shonte'?"

Shonte' picked up her phone and threw it at him. "That's what's wrong with me. I can't believe you did this to me."

Brooklyn looked at Shonte's phone and began reading all the tweets. "What the... Shonte' you believe this shit?" he said loudly. "Is this what you are all upset about?" A vein started throbbing in the middle of his forehead. Brooklyn was getting angry as hell.

"Well it obviously ain't for no other reason," she said.

"You in here passing out and throwing dishes at me because of some bullshit you read on the internet? You must be out your muthafuckin mind if you think I would do some dumb shit like get a bitch pregnant. I aint like your ex-husband. I'm a real nigga and I do real shit, so don't you ever in your life do no shit to me like you did tonight. Throwing glass and shit; passing out having a damn tantrum. That shit is for kids. We on some grown man and grown woman shit."

"Brooklyn, stop lying to me," Shonte' cried. "You are full of shit and I know you're lying. A baby Brooklyn, really? and I wouldn't have been throwing shit at you if you wouldn't have been getting bitches pregnant."

"No Shonte', look I just told you aint nobody having my baby," he leaned in close to Shonte' and whispered, "The only person I want to have my baby is you."

Brooklyn's phone started to buzz. He got a text message. Brooklyn read the text and immediately put the phone in his pocket, then continued to console Shonte'.

"Who was that?" Shonte' asked in a shaky teary voice.

"Look baby." Brooklyn gently grabbed Shonte' and held her in his arms. They both stayed quiet for a while, listening to each other's heartbeat. "I'm gonna be flying out tonight. I got some last-minute business I gotta take care of."

"Tonight?" Shonte' asked.

"Yes, and this cannot wait," he replied. Brooklyn pulled away from Shonte' and looked deeply into her brown eyes. "You know I love you. You are everything to me and you are all I have right now. I need you." He wiped the tears from her eyes with his thumb.

Shonte' glanced up at him as she lay against his chest. She noticed the cut on his forearm and gently rubbed her finger across it.

"Ah," he said with pain in his voice. "It still hurts, be careful girl."

"Well you deserved it Brooklyn. Don't think you can just rub the tears from my eyes and everything is going to be ok. I do love you but I refuse to be like those dumb ass women on those T.V. shows that stay with those men just for the money. Money is not that important to me and as soon as I feel like you are playing with my heart I will leave you Brooklyn and I mean that sincerely." She grabbed a bottle of peroxide and poured it on his open wound.

Brooklyn was getting turned on as she gently touched his wound. "You are the only person I want to carry my child," he said as he gazed into her beautiful brown eyes. Brooklyn began to rub his fingertips on the nape of her neck and softly spoke the words, "You are my dream girl and I would never put you at risk. I want you in my life forever." With every word he whispered his hands were rubbing gently over Shonte' s milky brown skin.

From the back of her neck, down her spine and all the way to her nice round bottom. He grabbed her aggressively and quietly asked, "Do you hear me?"

Shonte' didn't say a word, but her body told on her. She was shivering and shaking from the gentle touches of Brooklyn's fingertips. He then began to lick and nibble on her ear. "I asked you if you heard me?" He placed his hand between her thighs.

"Yes," She said abruptly. She felt the moisture between her legs coming out of her like a water fountain.

Brooklyn used his hands to put Shonte' in a place where she could no longer deny him. She closed her eyes, and all of a sudden, she couldn't remember why she was ever upset. Everywhere he put his hands made her body jolt in convulsions. He gently laid her on the floor and unbuckled his blinged-out belt.

Brooklyn looked at Shonte' like she was the most beautiful piece of artwork he had ever laid eyes on. He stood there for a moment, mesmerized by her beauty. "Damn, you're amazing."

Shonte' raised herself from the floor and grabbed him. He was aroused just by looking at her. Shonte' felt him growing in her hand. She softly placed her lips on his erect body; kissed and licked his erect skin until it was slippery. All Brooklyn could do was moan, and tell her how much he loved her. He put his hands on both sides of her head, and helped her along in the process.

"Damn girl I fucking love you. Please, whatever you do, don't stop. Oh my God! I love this shit right here."

Shonte' was going down on him like she had never done before. Brooklyn began to tremble. He stopped her right at that very moment by pulling her head away from his genitals. He lay her down on the floor, rubbed his hands over her body, and said, "I'm about to give you a baby right now."

He thrust inside of her. Shonte' gasped. He pulled back slowly and thrusted again. Slowly at first, then hard again. Shonte' was pulling away from him. "No. You not going nowhere," he commanded.

Brooklyn placed his body on top of her. She had no way out. He banged her body over and over and over again. "Yeah this is what you needed, right here. I fucking love you girl and you ain't going nowhere."

He gave her one final stroke and stayed there until he left his warm, milky substance inside of her.

"Yeah," he groaned.

Shonte' groaned his name with enjoyment and said, "Brooklyn baby it's all yours." They released simultaneously. Both of their hot sweaty bodies throbbed against one another.

Their hearts were racing rapidly and in tune with each other. Brooklyn mustered up enough strength to pull away, and lay alongside Shonte'. He grabbed her waist. They both closed their eyes, and basked in the moment. Brooklyn rubbed his thumb over Shonte's eyebrow and said, "Baby I gotta go."

"Go? Go Where?" she asked quizzically. "I just gotta go."

"No, I don't want you to leave," she demanded.

"Nah this can't wait. This is street business and it's got to be done today. This can't wait, but I will be back. You just keep my shit tight. Aight." Brooklyn got up, buckled his belt buckle and headed towards the front door.

Just as he stepped out of their eight-bedroom mini hotel, he got another text from Nikki Sullivan. This time, Brooklyn opened it, and began scanning the content of the previous message as well as this new one. Nikki was going in on him tonight, talking shit about pregnancies and sending him photos of baby bumps. She even had the audacity to request forty racks to keep her ass quiet. This bitch was crazy.

Brooklyn still didn't reply. He shook his head and mumbled to himself, "This bitch really don't know. Well, she gon' learn today."

Brooklyn stopped in his tracks and thought about Shonte'. He began to plot, which is something he hated to do to her, but he needed her to be on his team. He went back inside and peaked in the kitchen. Shonte' wasn't there. He went upstairs to their bedroom and saw her in the shower, and that's when he snuck into one of their beautiful guest rooms and quietly placed his phone on the bed, but not before deleting the messages and placing a lock on his phone.

He once again exited their wooden double doors and jumped into his Gray Mercedes G-Wagon, then proceeded to exit the golden gates of his estate.

Brooklyn always kept two phones. He opened the glove compartment and pulled out a trac phone. He placed a call to a longtime friend and pilot, Brian. The line cracked and a croaky voice was in his ear. "Hello?" The voice said.

"Yo B... B…Yo...wake up, I know it's late but we got some business to handle…Wake up B this gotta happen now, like right now."

"Aight Brook. I'm up." Brian was lying next to his girlfriend who was still naked from their interactions just moments before. The white bedding was only covering half of her body and her nice round Ebony bottom peeked out almost as if she had done it on purpose. Brian looked over at her while still speaking to Brooklyn and gave her bottom as soft smack. She inched closer to him and lay on his chest.

"There's something in it for you," Brooklyn said. "You know I always hook my boy up. The sky's the limit B, you hear me?" Brooklyn crossed over a bridge, still a little paranoid from what happened earlier that day.

He was paying attention to every car that drove behind him and passed him. His eyes danced from one mirror to the next – the left side view, rear view, right side view; front window. Brooklyn was very cautious about his movements. Being aware and paying attention has kept him out of prison for a lot of years and he wasn't about to change it up today. The city lights glared against the dark tinted windows as he passed through the city.

"Yeah, I got it. The sky's the limit," Brian replied, bringing him out of his daydream.

Brooklyn and Brian always spoke in code and never had any misunderstandings. Brian knew exactly what Brooklyn was referring to. "I'm hungry too B. Imma need one of them Philly cheese steaks, you feel me?"

"Hell yeah, I could go for a couple of those right about now."

"Aight, we on.

Brooklyn and Brian pulled up to the private jet strip at the same time. "I love coming out here," Brooklyn said. "The strip is always jet black like they just painted it and the way the lights shine against the tar makes me feel like I'm going somewhere special."

"Yeah that shit is dope. When you got money like you bro, I guess you get to see shit most people don't."

As Brooklyn and Brian were admiring the tar strip a plane was landing. It was loud and the wind started to blow excessively. Both Brian and Brooklyn looked up in amazement.

"I still don't see how these muthafuckas stay in the air, that shit blows my mind every time," Brooklyn said.

"It's all mathematics my brotha and if you like I can explain it to you," Brian said with a smirk.

"Nah we ain't got time for all that shit. Let's do this."

Brooklyn reached in his truck and grabbed a couple of Cuban cigars. "Here you go bro have one on me." They lit up the cigars together and took a moment to enjoy the amazing jet strip in front of them.

Brooklyn blew the smoke in the air and said, "Yo B. I appreciate you man, and this is for you." Brooklyn pulled out a brown paper bag from inside of his leather jacket and placed it in Brian's hand. The bag contained five-thousand dollars.

"Brook, you know you be doing too much sometimes. All of this is never necessary. I mean we been knowing each other since we was kids bro. I will do this shit for you no matter what. I mean all the shit we been through together. The jail time you helped me evade, helping my moms when she got cancer, and being my kids Godfather. Bro I got you no matter what."

"Nah... You my boy and loyalty is everything to me. If there's loyalty there's no deception, and no deception keeps Brooklyn a free man." He slapped Brian on the back of the shoulder. "So let's get these toys on this plane and handle this."

The pair walked over to his private storage area near the plane. Brooklyn opened the door and the smell of wood hit them both in the face. "I love that smell," Brooklyn said.

"Damn Brook. What you got up in all these crates?"

With the cigar still hanging from his mouth, he replied with a smirk, "I'm about to show you." Brooklyn opened one of the crates with the crowbar he grabbed from its hanger on the wall.

"What the fu..." Brian couldn't get his words out without losing his breath. He walked over to the box and pulled out a semi-automatic pistol. "Damn Brook. A Draco? What you tryna do? I haven't played like this in a long time." They were like two kids in a candy shop.

"Yeah that's for you and I'm about to rock with this long nose dirty dick. I'm gone be looking like Dirty Harry is this bitch. Matter of fact I'm about to grab two of these bitches." They grabbed the guns they wanted and put them into a gym bag.

Brooklyn and Brian strolled towards the fleer jet. The wind from the aircraft was strong and their clothes were flapping in the wind.

Brooklyn stepped onto the jet first and Brian was right behind him. It was decked out with tan leather interior, bucket-style seating and a full bar. Brian sat the bag of toys in one of the plush leather seats. Brooklyn poured himself a drink and buckled himself in.

Brian took his place as pilot and began pressing on the multi-colored display. "This is PJ227 preparing for takeoff, are we clear?" Brian continued with pilot jargon.

Brooklyn listened in but knew he couldn't make sense of it so he sat back relaxed and waited until they were at a comfortable altitude to move around.

Once they were in the sky, Brooklyn walked up to Brian and filled him in on what was going on. "Yo B? You remember that show we did in Philly a few months ago?"

"Yeah, I do, why? What's up?"

"So… after the show I hook up with this five-three, brown skin, blonde hair little pretty bitch. She was on me."

"Oh yeah… I remember. She was trying to give you that Becky in front of everybody."

"Exactly. That's her. First of all, this bitch gets on Twitter posting shit about she pregnant with my baby, taking pics of her belly and shit. Then the bitch sends me a text talking bout she wants forty racks to keep quiet. For one she was already talking so how she gonna blackmail me with the shit she already leaked. Two, it ain't mine. I had 2 jimmy's on that night and I pulled out."

"Bro, are you serious? Yeah, this shit has got to be dealt with quietly."

"See B, this is where they got me fucked up. They think I'm this stereotypical low budget brotha from the gutter. I'm from the gutter but I'm anything but typical. Now, I could've let some of this shit go and just handled it differently, but Shonte' found out and when I saw that look in her eyes it fucked me up B. So, we gotta put a handle on this amateur shit like yesterday."

"I got you Brook, but I got a couple hittas out there in Philly, we didn't even need to do all this."

"Nah! This shit's personal. This bitch causing problems at the castle. You know how it goes. If I don't handle this one, the word spreads like wildfire. Plus, it's been a minute since I got my hands dirty. I need this for me. I feel like I'm getting soft."

"Then we on. Sit back, relax and I will let you know when we arrive in Philly."

Brooklyn did just that. He lit up his fat Cuban cigar, poured himself a glass of Louis the thirteen that was stashed in the overhead compartment, and amped himself up for getting his hands dirty. "Ok. Nikki Sullivan, you woke up a real one. You have no idea what you have done," he said, as he gazed out at the darkness of the night.

"You just don't know."

*

Chapter 2: Philadelphia

When Brian and Brooklyn landed on the tar strip in Philadelphia, there was a black Lincoln town car with black tinted windows awaiting their arrival.

The driver was one of Brian's most trusted Comrades. Brian sat in the front passenger seat and Brooklyn climbed in the back. He was wearing an all-black hoodie, black jeans, and dark sunglasses.

Brian introduced his faithful Comrade. "Stacks, this is Brooklyn, Brooklyn this is Stacks."

"Nice to meet you man, thanks for hooking a brother up," Brooklyn said.

Stacks dapped Brooklyn. "Likewise. And hey, anyone who fucks with Brian is a friend of mine."

"Stacks, we're gonna head out to the east side. You know over there by the train tracks? I think you used to date a chick that lived out that way."

"Oh yeah, I know where you talking about. Stacey used to live over there. I wonder what ever happened to her."

"Oh shit," Brian said. "Don't be trying to rekindle some old-ass romance. We got binness bro."

Stacks gave a sincere smile. Brian handed him a brown paper bag, gave him a handshake, and they proceeded to their destination.

*

In a space black as night and the heat of her panting breath, Shonte flopped around like a fish out of water. She felt confused and out of place. She had no idea where she was. After fidgeting around with several unsuccessful attempts to free herself, she saw a latch and prayed it would somehow free her from the trifling space she had found herself in. She pulled the latch and the trunk went flying open. She gasped with relief. "Thank God," she mumbled.

She climbed out of the trunk and looked around. Where the hell am I? She could hear screaming and terror coming from behind her. She turned around and started to walk towards it.

"I know this is a bad idea," she uttered. "I can just feel it."

She glanced over and walked toward an apartment building where the screams were coming from. They were getting louder with every step she took. Shonte' ducked down and looked inside the tiny apartment window and couldn't believe what she was seeing.

"No! Brooklyn! Please! I'm sorry I lied. It's not your baby!"

"I know it's not Bitch." Brooklyn pointed the long-barrel gun at Robert's head.

"Please. Please don't shoot him," Nikki cried.

Brooklyn walked over to Nikki. "I know that baby ain't mine. I stay strapped with two jimmies bitch. The only reason you got this dick is because you fucked your home girl for me. I gave your stupid ass a thousand dollars just so this shit wouldn't happen and you tried to fuckin play me for a sucka. You see, you took me for one of them studio niggas. You thought I was all talk. You better check the resume'. This shit right here, I fucking love it, and I miss it for real. I'm that guy that will blaze the whole fucking block just to prove my point. Now whose fucking idea was this?"

Nikki was crying hysterically. She and her lover were both tied to wooden chairs. Her white T-Shirt was soaking wet from the tears that were spewing from her eyes like rain.

Robert groaned as Brian hit him with the Draco. Blood splattered across the floor. Robert was trying to slide away, still tied to the chair. Brian kicked him, then hit him again with the gun. Robert screamed loudly and spat a few of his teeth out. Brian stood back and took aim.

Nikki screamed, "No! I'm sorry. I'm so sorry. Please don't shoot him, I will give you the money back. I will do whatever you want. Please... Please. Just please – whatever it is, I will do it. Don't shoot him."

"Fuck you," Robert yelled to Brian.

"What you say to me?"

"I said fuck you."

Brian gave a devious smile. "Are you sure you wanna say that to me? The man standing before you with a gun cocked at your brains? I'm going to give you a chance to apologize, even though my trigger finger is itching. I'm still a good guy, and I want to be merciful. Robert bloodied and still tied to the chair.

"This can't be happening. Robert, just shut up. Just shut the fuck up!" The last of Nikki's sanity had finally left her.

Brian was unusually calm in contrast. It was almost chilling. "Now, I am going to untie you and I want you to apologize. Plus, I like to fight fair." Brian did as he said he would.

"Fuck you," Robert said. He spat in Brian's face and took off running towards the door.

Brooklyn immediately sprang into action and pulled out both of his long nose-dirty dicks and aimed right at Roberts's legs. Two crisp shots punctured the momentary silence and seemed to drain the world of all its remaining hope.

Robert screamed as he fell to the floor. He hollered out in a tone so frail that the crisp words of coldness he spat only seconds ago were revealed as the double bluffs they were. "You shot me in my kneecaps. Get help, please!" Blood was spilling from his body rapidly.

"See what you made me do bitch?"

"Damn Brooklyn," Brian said. "I wanted to try out the Draco. I can't believe this dude spit in my face."

"Oh my God! Oh my God! Oh my God! Please..." Nikki begged.

Brooklyn walked back over to Nikki and continued his conversation as if he hadn't just put two holes in her boyfriend. "Money? Is that what you think this is about? This ain't about no fucking money. This is about the disrespect. Putting my name in the streets and asso- ciating me with bullshit. How about you use that money to buy ya boy a new grill. And some legs, for that matter"

Brooklyn kicked Robert again and again with his steel toe boot. Robert moaned in agony, as he lay in his own pool of blood. His breathing was getting faint and he was going in and out of consciousness. Nikki sat there slumped over, slobbering as snot ran from her nose into her mouth.

Brooklyn walked over to Robert and whispered to him, "I know this was your idea and Ima tell you like this, I'm never out of reach. Just because you see me on T.V. don't mean I won't let you meet me." Brooklyn kicked Robert in the ribs once more and said to Brian, "Let's get out of here. The police gon be showing up soon."

Brooklyn looked at Nikki and shook his head with sheer disappointment. He cut her loose and said, "That's what you do to your brother." Nikki immediately ran to Robert and held him.

Brooklyn and Brian walked out the front door of the tiny apartment, leaving a trail of blood behind them.

Shonte' woke in a pool of sweat and began gasping for breath.

"Not again."

She ran to the medicine cabinet and took a pill to calm her nerves. She mumbled to herself as she walked, "I can't believe this. It's happening again. I thought I had gotten rid of those stupid stupid dreams. I can't do this again. I just can't. These dreams are going to drive me crazy." Shonte' started to cry. "Why is this happening and what does this mean?" She asked herself. "I thought those days were all behind me."

Shonte' picked up her phone and called Brooklyn to warn him of her dream. She could hear his phone ringing in the other room. "Damnit," she said.

He left his phone here on purpose, she thought, just as he always does. Shonte' remembered overhearing Brooklyn talking about how he never takes his phone with him while handling street business. His voice replayed in her mind. "You know that ain't nothing but a tracking device."

She was all too familiar with these types of dreams and she knew it would soon come to fruition. She began to worry, and could only pray for the safe return of her lover. This was a new aspect of their relationship. Shonte' could handle the girls, the fame, and all the extra attention, but worrying about his safety, and wondering if she would ever see him again, was not something she was prepared for.

*

Chapter 3: Brooklyn Is Home

Brooklyn arrived home just as the sun was gleaming right above the rooftop of their mansion. He cruised up the driveway, waved to the security guard and parked the Mercedes truck beside Shonte's SL 500 Mercedes Benz. He quietly opened the large wooden doors and tiptoed upstairs.

As he opened the bedroom door, he leaned inside. Shonte' was sleeping quietly, and the sun was shining beautifully on her bronze skin. "Damn, I'm a lucky man," he whispered.

Brooklyn got in the bed and lay down beside Shonte'. He kissed her on the back of her neck and gently grabbed her waist. Shonte' grabbed his hand with a sense of relief. She was glad he was back home lying beside her, in her arms as he should be.

Later that morning Shonte' woke up before Brooklyn and started making breakfast for him. Chicken and cheese omelet with avocado. The room was filled with a delicate aroma of chicken and cheese that only she could put together. Shonte' turned on the eighty-inch flat screen TV, and that's when she saw it.

It was a newsflash from CNN about a man and woman brutally attacked, shot and left for dead, at an apartment in Philadelphia. The description of the victims was just like her dream the night before. She became frightened and began to panic all over again. She bit her bottom lip so hard it began to bleed.

I need to sit down; my head is starting to hurt, she thought. Shonte' sat down at the kitchen table and put a cold rag on her head to try and calm herself down.

Brooklyn made his way downstairs with a smile on his face. He looked at Shonte' with love in his eyes, and said, "I see you made my favorite. Thank you, baby." He kissed her lips gently, and said, "My love for you is very intense. I hope you don't ever try to leave me because that would be a problem," he said with a devilish grin.

Shonte' made Brooklyn's plate and sat down at the table beside him. "You're in a rather cheerful mood this morning. Why are you so happy?" Shonte' was trying to hide her anxiety, but Brooklyn was picking up on something. "So, I tried to call you last night but you left your phone here."

Brooklyn looked at her with a frown on his face. "What's up with you? Are you still tripping about that baby shit? And to answer your question, you already know I don't take my phone with me when I'm handling street shit. Why were you trying to call me? Did something happen?"

"No. I just couldn't sleep. I tossed and turned and had a few nightmares that scared the shit out of me."

"For real? After I put all that on you, you couldn't sleep?"

Shonte' looked at Brooklyn, expecting him to tell her what happened last night. She was puzzled with his reaction and unresponsiveness.

"What? Why are you looking at me like that? What's up with you?" he asked.

"Well I was watching the news this morning and there was a story about this man and this woman who got beat up and shot in Philly."

"Ok, and that bothers you because?"

"No reason. The story just grabbed my attention," she said.

"Well ungrab it," he said angrily. "I don't know why you be watching that shit anyway. If they ain't talking money, then it's a waste of time. And my time is priceless." He took a forkful to his mouth and swallowed it in one gulp. "So, did the police catch the people that did it?" He asked between bites.

"I don't think so. The police are investigating, but they would only say that it didn't appear to be a robbery because nothing was taken, and the witnesses aren't saying anything."

"Humph," Brooklyn mumbled. "Why does that story interest you so much?" He felt his body temperature rising.

"I don't know Brooklyn, I just had a really bad dream last night, and I'm hoping it's not true." Shonte' was still terrified and trembled when she thought of her dream.

"Here you go with those dreams again. Remember we talked about this. If you ever dream about me and it ain't good, I don't even want to know about it. I can handle myself. Baby you worry way too much. I can take care of you and keep you safe. I know your ex- husband couldn't do that for you, but I am all you will ever need. Believe that."

Shonte' stared at Brooklyn as he continued to speak, his lips were moving but she wasn't listening. She just kept staring at his body, as if she was trying to memorize every scar and every tattoo. She started to bite down on her bottom lip and the memory of them making love began to play over in her mind.

She was getting turned on. Shonte' started thinking about the dream she had about Brooklyn beating another man and it was getting her aroused. She felt herself getting hot and bothered.

"Shonte'? Hello? Are you listening to me?"

Shonte' snapped out of it and was brought back to reality. "Huh, yeah… yes babe, I'm listening."

"No, you weren't, but it's all good because I know that look baby."

"What look?" Shonte' asked.

"That look. Baby, I study everything about you. I know shit you do that you don't even know you do. I can see you, but you can't see you. I always know exactly what you want and need. You don't ever have to say a word."

Shonte' was wearing only a t-shirt and a thong. This was all he needed to get him going. Brooklyn hopped up from the table and pounced on Shonte' like a tiger attacking its prey. He pushed all the dishes from the counter to the floor, picked Shonte' up and laid her on the island in their kitchen. "Wait, don't move," he said. "I'll be right back."

He turned on the intercom that played music directly from his phone and programmed it to play R. Kelly Sex in the Kitchen. Brooklyn returned to Shonte', who obeyed Brooklyn's command and hadn't moved an inch.

While the music played in the background, they tried to experience every moment in the song. R-Kelly was doing his thing. "Over by the stove, put you on the counter by the butter rolls."

That's exactly where Shonte' and Brooklyn were. They indulged in each other. Kissing hard and passionately, and then taking their time, slowly and succulently. Their breath was heavy with excitement and their hearts were beating to the rhythm of the song.

Each time Brooklyn thrust inside of her she rhythmically gave it back to him. It was almost like their bodies were in a tennis match. Both their bodies raced to catch the other's essence, so they could force it back to the other side. Their pace was slow when necessary and speedy when the rhythm called for it.

Brooklyn had never met anyone who made him feel like this. He stopped in motion as he lay on top of her and asked if she loved him.

"Yes, baby I love you."

He began again, slowing moving himself inside her. Shonte' felt an explosion and screamed. Brooklyn moaned and she screamed again and yelled his name. They were loud enough for the neighbors to hear.

Their passion for each other almost made them forget where they were. Shonte' and Brooklyn were so wrapped up in each other they didn't even hear the doorbell ringing.

They continued, but were soon brought down from their soul explosion by a tapping on the kitchen window. "What is that? Oh my God that looks like the cops," Shonte' said.

Brooklyn glanced out the window. "It sure is," he said. He looked at the cop, smiled and started going in harder on Shonte'.

She tried to speak but every time she tried to utter any words Brooklyn gave it to her harder and deeper, not allowing a syllable to exit mouth. "I'm not about to let nothing stop me today baby." He licked Shonte' from her breasts down to her belly button, and then moved between her legs.

Shonte's body began to shake uncontrollably. First her left leg, then both. Then she screamed. The passion exhaled from her loins like a lioness on her first kill.

Shonte' closed her eyes and acted as if there wasn't currently a cop watching them have sex through the kitchen window.

"Hey," the cop said. "I can see you in there."

Brooklyn continued to kiss Shonte', and without losing any focus on her, he gave the cop the middle finger and continued. "Do you love me?" Brooklyn asked.

Shonte' was in a zone and didn't reply. At least not until Brooklyn gave her a long hard thrust. "Yes," she yelled. "Yes, baby I love you." The cop was still watching, and yelled through the window, "That's ok, we'll be back. You just don't go anywhere."

Shonte' and Brooklyn continued to indulge in each other until they were both tired and out of breath.

Once they could breathe again, Shonte' asked Brooklyn, "What did the police want, babe?"

"I don't know, maybe they just wanted to watch you and me," Brooklyn said with a devilish smile.

"Brooklyn, are you in trouble?"

"Baby, don't worry. I'm black, I'm young, and I'm rich. The police will always be at our door for something." He gently kissed her on the forehead.

As Brooklyn and Shonte' cleaned all the broken glass from their moment of passion, Brooklyn's phone started to buzz. It was a text message with a video link. It was Nikki Sullivan.

"Babe, check this out, you gotta see this."

The video started with Nikki saying, "I want to apologize for the statements I made about Brooklyn. My boyfriend Robert told me to do it since I was already pregnant, and I shared a moment with Brooklyn. Again, I apologize to Brooklyn if I have caused any turmoil in his life. I am not pregnant with his baby."

"And what *moment* is she talking about Brook?"

"Baby are you serious? This woman just apologized and posted this all over the internet and you still want to be mad?" Shonte' gave Brooklyn a serious look of shock, as if she couldn't believe he was asking her that. "Ok baby, look. I had a show in Philly and I let her give me some head. I'm sorry, but babe, what did you want me to do? I got hard and plus I was loaded. Damn baby, I just want to make you happy."

"That makes no sense Brooklyn. Just because you got hard doesn't mean it wasn't cheating."

"Don't sweat the small shit. Baby, I'm a rapper. Women love me, and I love women. I'm a man and I will always be attracted to other women, but I got the Queen of the Nile right here. Just because I'm attracted to them broads don't mean I'm trying to replace my Queen. You got me baby?"

"Yeah Brook, I got you." Shonte' still wasn't satisfied with Brooklyn's answer, but she did love him and wanted to make it work, so she put it out of her mind and kissed Brooklyn on the forehead.

"What's up with your column? Why haven't you been writing like you used to? You seem to be kind of bored around here. If you stay home thinking about what I'm doing all day, you gonna end up losing your mind. You need something to do. Maybe *you* need a ba- by."

Shonte's eyes got really big. "Maybe so," she said.

*

Chapter 4: Shonte's Baby

Shonte' had never mentioned to Brooklyn that it was even a possibility she could be pregnant with Ronny's baby. Ronny's words kept running through her head: "You are gonna have my baby." Shonte' could see the goosebumps appearing on her arms, and chills started to run down her spine.

Brooklyn had left for one of his shows, and it was the perfect time for her to get this pregnancy test over and done with. Shonte' raced up the gallery stairs to take the test. As her soft round bottom sat on the cold porcelain stool, she couldn't help but think about Brooklyn. The anxiety started to set in and her body temperature was rising. She could feel the sweat starting to bead up on her forehead.

Her mind began to drift as she sat there staring at the pregnancy test. What if I am pregnant? What if it's Ronny's? Will Brooklyn leave me? Shonte' was making herself hysterical with all the what ifs and maybes. She was so anxious that she had bitten her nails down to the skin.

"Oh my God this is taking too long," she said to herself. "This is the longest five minutes of my life."

As she paced back and forth across the wooden floor, each creek sounded like it was saying, "Ronny, you are the father." She paused for a moment, took a deep breath, and slowly stepped into the highly vaulted bathroom that looked like something fresh out of a home magazine strictly focusing on million-dollar bathrooms.

Shonte' was so nervous about the test results that she almost threw up. She even gagged a few times. Her hands were shaking tremendously, and her heart began to beat at an excessive pace. The pregnancy test had one line and a shallow second line. "What does that mean?"

Shonte' rustled through the box for the instructions. After carefully reading the entire thing, she learned that the test results were inconclusive.

Shonte' tried every single pregnancy test she had and they all came back inconclusive. "What am I gonna do now?" she mumbled.

"Baby, I'm home." His voice echoed against the walls as if it was a recording studio. Brooklyn was home early.

"Damn he's home early." Shonte' anxiously tried to get rid of all of the pregnancy tests. Shit, what am I going to do? If Brooklyn finds out I'm taking a pregnancy test, he's going to be asking so many questions. Just as she was thinking this, Brooklyn walked in.

"What are you doing?" he asked. Shonte' was holding all of the pregnancy tests that she had managed to force into a plastic shopping bag behind her back. "What's that behind your back? What are you trying to hide?"

Shonte's eyes got big, and she managed to get the words out. "N-nothing."

"Girl, stop playing. There's something you're holding behind your back." Brooklyn stepped behind her, grabbed the bag, and looked inside. "Baby," he said with excitement. "Are we pregnant? Are we having a baby? I thought you were on the pill. Oh well, damn, all of that. I see you took a few tests already, so what does this line and half of a line mean?"

"They all came back inconclusive Brook... I don't know if I'm pregnant or not."

"How can you not know? It's a pregnancy test. You pee on the stick, and it tells you if you are pregnant or not."

The floor swayed beneath Shonte's feet. She placed her hand on her forehead, and then her knees began to buckle.

Brooklyn caught her just before she hit the floor. "Nope. Don't be falling out with my seed in you. I got you baby, and little baby." Brooklyn picked Shonte' up and carried her to the king-size mattress that he had gotten custom-made just for them. He laid Shonte' on the bed, kissed her forehead, and whispered, "Baby, I'm gonna take care of us. I promise. No more games, no more women. Just you, me, and Jr." He stroked her forehead as he spoke. "Baby, I got us."

"Brooklyn, the results were inconclusive. I may not even be pregnant, and here you are making all these plans about a baby that may not even exist. I wish you would just stop."

"Wait, what? I'm not even going to respond to that silly-ass comment. I'm just gonna blame that on the pregnancy. I will ask you this though, did you miss your period?"

"Yes Brooklyn, I did," she said.

"Okay, then that solves it. You're pregnant." Brooklyn climbed into bed next to Shonte' and laid his head on her belly as if he were listening for a heartbeat. "I'm gonna call him BK. Nah, that sounds like a burger or some shit. What about Dillon? Then we can call him Dope Dillon. Nah, I'm just kidding. Ok… ok… I got it! We are gonna name him Majesty. Boom, that part. That's it!"

Brooklyn went on and on about the sports he would play with his son, and the clothes he would buy for him. As he went on and on and on, Shonte' dozed off a little but could still hear Brooklyn making plans for a child that may not even exist.

She opened her eyes slightly, enough to see he was still resting on her belly. I wish he would just leave and go away so I can think. All these crazy plans he's making are driving me insane. I need a moment to clear my head, she thought.

Shonte' rested for a moment and was quickly woken by Brooklyn asking if she was asleep. He never waited for her to respond. His voice was shallow and she couldn't understand what he was saying with all the clutter in her mind. Suddenly, it hit her. A shadowing voice saying, "You're gonna have my baby". Only this time, it wasn't Brooklyn's voice.

Shonte' woke, breathing heavily.

Oh my God Ronny. Her mind was racing with thoughts of Ronny.

*

Chapter 5: Your Majesty

Shonte' really wasn't sure if she was actually pregnant, but Ronny's daunting voice kept playing over and over in her head. *What if I am pregnant? What if it's Ronny's? What am I going to tell Brooklyn? This would devastate him.* I would have to be a crazy person to have Ronny's baby and try to pass it off as Brooklyn's. This is some fucked up shit and I can't be a part of it. Nope. No way, no how. I refuse to be a part of some freak show.

Shonte' sat in the waiting room, anxiously awaiting her name to be called. Waiting rooms always made her nervous. It reminded her of when she was a child and her father made her see a shrink. Her palms became sweaty and she began to perspire. All of those old emotions came rolling right back to her. Her leg shook so fast and hard that she knocked over the magazines beside her.

"Sorry," she said, and she stacked the magazines back on the table. The other people in the room looked at her strangely.

Finding out if she was pregnant or not was stressful enough, but sitting in a waiting room was making things a whole lot worse. What could she do about it? This needed to happen and it needed to happen now. Brooklyn was on tour with a few shows to do, so the time was now or never.

"Ms. Smith?"

"Finally," Shonte' mumbled. "Yes, that's me." Shonte' quickly jumped up and met the nurse at the door. The nurse guided her through the office.

"Go to room two please," the nurse said with a smile. Shonte' whisked right into the room and the nurse was right behind her. "So, you're here for a pregnancy test, correct?"

"Yes, I took a few tests at home but they came back inconclusive. I'm not sure why they even make pregnancy tests if they can't tell you for sure if you're pregnant or not. I wish I could get my money back. It was a complete waste of my time." Shonte' showed her frustration with the entire system by rolling her eyes at the nurse.

"Ok, well, we can resolve that for you today. Here's a cup. Take this in the restroom with you and when you're done place the urine sample on the table. Then wait for your name to be called."

"You mean I have to wait again? That must be all you people get paid for, telling people to wait around all day." Shonte' stormed into the bathroom and slammed the door. Everyone in the room jolted and whispered about her.

Although she was unwilling, Shonte' followed the nurse's orders to a tee. She peed in the cup, placed it on the table, and then took a seat in the waiting room. As she glanced over to the stack of reading material that these people deemed entertainment, she saw a magazine that had a daunting headline printed in big black letters across the front page.

Brooklyn's Baby Mama Drama

As if she wasn't already going through enough, she was again faced with this Nikki Sullivan situation. Shonte' hesitatingly walked over to the magazine. She picked it up, sat down, and decided to read the gossip-filled propaganda.

With everything that was going on, Shonte' was on edge. Without even realizing it, she had bitten her nails down to the cuticle again and this time they were bleeding. Her left leg was shaking uncontrollably and all she could think about was getting out of that horrible room.

The woman seated next to her noticed what she was reading and asked, "So, do you think it's true? Do you think it really is his baby, and she's just lying to cover for him?"

Shonte' was enraged and felt violated by this stranger's question. She sat there for a moment and stared at the woman, giving her the evil eye.

Shonte' was growing more and more infuriated by the minute. Her eyebrows were scrunched down, and her lips were pressed together. She took a deep breath and calmly said to the woman, "I'm sure it's not his."

"What makes you so sure?"

Shonte's leg was shaking erratically, and she was gritting her teeth. She stood in front of the woman with her fist balled up, and right as she was about to show the woman why she was so sure with her fist, a voice broke the silence.

"Ms. Smith?" The nurse's voice came into the room like a bell-ringing at the end of a boxing match. Just as well, too, because it had almost been lights out for that broad sitting next to her.

Shonte' took a deep breath, and her shoulders dropped. She looked at the woman in front of her and rolled her eyes. "Yes, that's me."

"Step back here, the doctor will see you now."

Shonte' made her way back behind the doctor's walls and once again into room two. She entered the room, sat down, and began waiting – again. The entire process was starting all over again. The nervousness, the anticipation. So many thoughts ran through her mind about Brooklyn and Ronny. About the decisions she was going to have to make.

I hate Ronny, and I know it will be all bad if I have his baby. I just can't allow this to be.

Next, she thought about how long she had been at that doctor's office just for a pregnancy test. Shonte' found herself chewing on her nails again. "This entire process is so stupid," she mumbled to herself. "I was just in here. They could have just kept me right here, but no."

"Hi, Ms. Smith," the doctor said with an excited tone as she entered the room, "I have your results, and congratulations, you're pregnant. I'm so happy for you. I'm going to prescribe you some prenatal vitamins to keep you and the baby healthy. Here's your prescription."

Shonte' could hear the words coming out of the doctor's mouth but she wasn't paying attention to her at all. The words were drowned out with Ronny's daunting voice, and Brooklyn's excitement about having a child. She tried to stand up but her legs were like rubber, and she fell to the floor.

"Oh my God, Miss Smith? Are you ok?"

When she came to, the doctor stood over her. "Yes, I'm okay." But clearly, she wasn't.

Shonte' began to feel as if she were underwater. Her ears were plugged; she could only vaguely hear the doctors and the nurses around her, and it seemed as if they were moving in slow motion. They picked her up and helped her to a chair.

"I'm fine. I just need some water. I'll be fine," she said.

"Are you sure?" the doctor asked.

"Yes, I'm sure," she replied, and just then, Shonte' vomited all over the doctor's shoes.

"Oh my God, I am so sorry. I guess it's from the baby." Shonte' grabbed some tissues and wiped her mouth. "Again, I am so sorry, but trust me, I am fine." Shonte' stood up, and while slightly bent over, she exited the doctor's office.

"Wait," the doctor exclaimed. You're going to need this." She handed Shonte' the prescription and said, "Once again, congratulations." The doctor gazed down at her shoes, which were covered in vomit, with disgust, but for some reason, she just couldn't let Shonte' leave like that. She grabbed a towel from one of the other waiting rooms, wiped the vomit from her red bottoms, and caught up to Shonte'.

"Wait. I know this is a lot to take in, and you probably have a thousand questions right now, but I want to help. I do have other patients to tend to, but I couldn't let you leave without at least letting you know that if you have any further questions, don't hesitate to ask. You can also speak to the nurses on your way out if there is something you would prefer to discuss with them."

The doctor gave Shonte' a few samples of prenatal vitamins and then made her way back to her patients.

As Shonte' made her way back to the car, she could feel her heart starting to beat swiftly. All she could think about was how damaged Brooklyn would be if she shared this with him. How is this even possible?

Shonte' didn't know how it was possible that she could be pregnant with Brooklyn's child. I've been taking my birth control. I missed a day or two, but they should still be working. No thoughts brought any clarity. At least none except the unthinkable. Oh my God, what if... What if it's not his?

She immediately called her best friend Mo.

"Hey Tay, what's going on with you? I was just thinking about you. You good?"

"Mo. Do you remember when I told you about the time Ronny snuck into the house and had sex with me, and I thought it was Michael?"

"Damn Bish.... Hi to you too...Yeah, my life is good. Tyrone made the basketball team, and he's going to a division one high school this year...but you know that's just how I'm doing. Thanks for asking."

"I'm so sorry Mo. I should have asked, but my life is turning upside down right now, and I have no idea what to do. I feel like I'm losing my mind," Shonte' said.

"Shit, you probably are; you know you ain't always been wrapped too tight. Plus, all that shit Michael put you through with that nasty- ass divorce. I would have lost my mind, too. Sometimes, we all lose it a little bit, but we gone be alright. Anyway, what's got you all crazy this time? Is it that Brooklyn and baby shit? If so, I would be glad to beat that little bitch's ass. I ain't had a real get down in a minute."

"No, from the looks of it, she's been taken care of."

"Oh well, in that case, on to the next. Why were you asking about that old shit with Ronny? Yeah, I do remember. Why, what's going" on?

"Well I wasn't using birth control and now I'm pregnant. Mo, I don't know if Ronny is the father or if it's Brooklyn."

Monique gasped. "Oh my God. What are you going to do?" "First, I'm going to the prison to visit Ronny. I need answers. I can't just continue living my life with all of these what ifs.

I will call you and let you know what happens." "You better call me back this time. Yo ass always say that shit, and you don't never call back."

"Ok, Mo. I will. I promise." With one click, the line went dead.

*

When Shonte' arrived at the prison, she wasn't sure if she was on the official visitor's list, but she decided to try her luck anyway. Shonte' remembered how grueling the process was while trying to visit an inmate. She thought about when she had to visit a cousin, and the experience was less than pleasant. After standing in line to get inside, waiting for your name to be called, and passing through the metal detectors, you were greeted with angry officers and rooms so dark they made outer space look light. Shonte' said, "It's almost as if they don't want anyone visiting."

After more than an hour in the waiting room, the guard yelled, "Visitor for Ronny Turner!"

"Finally," Shonte' said with relief. She bolted to her feet and approached the woman guard who inspected her clothing.

"This is too revealing," the guard said. "Take this pass and go to room two-two-seven and change into something less form fitting." Already frantic about being at the prison and working against the clock, Shonte' knew she had to make this quick. She swiftly made it through the drab halls of the prison and dashed straight into room two-two-seven.

"Hi, the guards sent me here to find something less revealing. Can you help? I'm kind of in a hurry. I need something in a size ten."

"Sure, and I'm sorry they sent you away. They always do things like that. I have just the thing." The woman browsed the rack and found a loose-fitting dress that was a perfect size ten.

"Yes! Thank you," Shonte' exclaimed with relief.

She raced into the bathroom, changed her clothes, and dashed back down to security, where she once again had to get scanned and checked.

"Next," the guard shouted. Shonte' passed through the metal detector and made her way down the hall towards D-Block, where Ronny was being held.

When Shonte' arrived in D-Block, she was greeted by another guard. She flashed her pass, and the guard escorted her to the area where Ronny was waiting. As she journeyed down the halls, a memory of her cousin who was killed in prison started to creep into her mind. She shed a few tears as they walked. "Are we almost there?" she asked in a demanding tone.

"Right here," the guard replied.

Shonte entered a room that was more like a breakroom than a holding cell. She stood there for a moment, stunned. She was frozen, unable to move, as the thoughts of their last night together started to formulate in her mind.

As she stepped further into the room Ronny looked up at her to see who his visitor was. Judging by his jaw dropping response, he was extremely surprised. Shonte' was the last person he expected to be paying him a visit.

"I knew it was a good idea to keep your name on that visitor's list. I knew one day you'd show up." He licked his lips and raised his eyebrows in her direction, this time in a way that simulated excitement instead of surprise. "You miss me, don't you? You miss me rubbing my hands between your thighs and making you scream. You miss how my tongue made you shiver…"

"Will you knock it off?" Shonte' cut him off mid-sentence. "The only thing that missed was the bullet that I should have put in your head." She put her two fingers to Ronny's head in the shape of a gun. "Click-click. Boom!" she said.

"If you really wanted me dead, Shonte', you would have done it. You had every opportunity that night in the hotel room. Fact of the matter is, there is something just as sick and sadistic about you that it is about me and you thrive in it.

"Did you forget what you did to me? Did you forget what you did to Brooklyn? Never mind, I know you didn't forget it. I came here to ask you one question and one question only. Was that really you that night in the shower with me?"

Ronny stood up. Standing over Shonte', cracking his neck on the left side and then on the right. He cracked his knuckles and gazed at Shonte' as if he was looking through her. He licked his lips and rubbed her eyebrow ever so gently, and replied, "Well, now, Miss Shonte' wants an answer. Sounds like you need something from me. Good baby, I need something from you too. You see, since I was a big time NFL player before I got in here, the guards let me do whatever I want. All I have to do is say the word."

Shonte' took a huge gulp and tried to hide the fact that she was extremely frightened by his response. She slowly inched further and further away from him inconspicuously.

"How about you take off all your clothes, lay on that bench, open your legs, and let me see how bad you really wanna know."

"Believe me, it's not that serious," she replied.

Inside, Shonte' wanted to ball up like a fetus, but she couldn't let Ronny know that she was getting more and more uncomfortable at an alarming rate. On the outside, she showed no fear. With a calm and non-threatening demeanor, she said, "You couldn't even handle me when you had me." Shonte' tossed her hair in a flirty manner.

"Oh, but I think it is that serious," he said. "See Shonte', you are more like me than you'd like to admit." He signaled for the guards to leave.

"Where are you going? Come back. You can't leave me here alone with this maniac." Shonte's previous attempts at appearing calm had just been rendered useless because now all of that pent-up fear was flooding out of her like water from a burst fire hydrant.

Ronny sat on the table in front of her. He softly brushed her hair behind her ear and began whispering into it, "I satisfy you in ways beyond your deepest imagination." He leaned in closer and softly tasted her skin. "How are your dreams coming?" he asked as he slowly withdrew.

"Funny you should ask. Ever since I eliminated you from my life, they suddenly ceased. What a coincidence. Wouldn't you agree?" Shonte' was speaking as if she wasn't the least bit spooked. Inside, her stomach was a seesaw.

"Don't lie. You and I both know how this works. The moment you become dissatisfied sexually, your dreams and prophecies begin to forecast in your mind. I can tell from the heat coming from your body that being in this room alone with me is turning you on. I know you have had a fantasy or two about fucking me right here, right now." Ronny leaned in closer. "Come on baby, what's stopping you?"

Shonte' didn't say a word. She got up to walk away, but Ronny grabbed her, put his hands between her legs and threw her against the wall. He placed his hand perfectly into her pants and rubbed fast and hard. Shonte' screamed for the guards but it came out more like a moan.

Ronny had her pinned against the wall. "Now there you go. That's my girl." He released his grip and backed away from her. He put his fingers in his mouth. "Damn, I forgot how good you taste."

"You think just because you are the only one that has ever given me an exhilarating orgasm with your mouth that I'm just supposed to forget about the hell you put me through? Ok. So, I like to cum. What woman doesn't? That doesn't mean that I am in love with you Ronny. You got it all twisted. The things you can do with your mouth will make the average woman fall victim to your extraordinary talent, and although I love how you make me feel, I live in the real- world, Ronny."

He signaled the guards to return with a brief hand gesture and said, "Yes, that was me at your house that night. And yes, I placed my seed inside you. So, when I get out of here, I expect ya'll to be waiting for me. We're family now." A smirk followed his words. "I love you." He smacked her ass and allowed the guard to handcuff him.

"Hey bro, if you need a few more minutes, I can work that out for you," the guard said as he prepared to escort Ronny back to the cell.

"Nah, I think we're done here for today. She'll be back."

The guard opened the door to the room and allowed Ronny to walk in front of him. He escorted him down the long halls of the dreary prison. Shonte' snared at Ronny as he slowly exited her presence and was still confused about how she was feeling.

Shonte' didn't budge from her seat. She was still in disbelief about what had just occurred. She was shivering with delight from the convulsions her body felt, but mentally, she was terrorized.

As she made her way back down the halls and past the heavily guarded cells, Shonte' didn't know if she was afraid or pleased. Scared or happy. Petrified or joyful. Her emotions were all over the place, and at this point, she felt like she was losing more of her mind by the minute.

What's wrong with me? She asked herself.

Once she made it to the car, she just sat there in the driver's seat, thinking about the excitement she had just enjoyed with Ronny and the betrayal she felt toward Brooklyn. All of the emotions overtook her and she let out a loud cry.

She banged her hand against the steering wheel and yelled, "Why, God, why? Why do I have this horrible curse?" During her emotional breakdown, she got a FaceTime call from Brooklyn.

"Fuck!" She exclaimed.

Shonte' didn't answer Brooklyn's call. She was too emotional, and she couldn't let Brooklyn see the tears in her eyes. Seconds later, she got a text.

Hey baby, trying to call you. Pick up.

Still, she didn't respond.

She knew exactly what needed to be done. She thought about everything she could lose with Brooklyn. She was finally happy and would do anything to stay that way, but she knew that if Brooklyn ever found out that it was even a possibility the baby could be Ronny's, she would lose his love forever.

She had a decision to make. Keep the baby and risk Ronny stalking her for the rest of her life, or abort the baby and continue her fairytale life with Brooklyn. The decision was easy.

Or so she thought.

*

Chapter 6: The Big Reveal

Sometimes, life gives you lemons. And you know what they say: when life gives you lemons, you make lemonade. But what do you make when life gives you the seed of another man? What do you do when you find yourself pregnant by a man who isn't your boyfriend?

Well, in that instance, you don't make lemonade; you make yourself cry at the terrible decisions you just made and drag your ass out of the abortion clinic before anyone had any chance of knowing you were ever there.

Only that thought turned out to be the opposite of Shonte's reality.

As she stepped down the back steps, the sea of white blinding light swarmed her like a bunch of pissed-off bees. *Shit. The paparazzi already? This can't be happening.*

"Is it true that you and Nikki Sullivan were both pregnant with Brooklyn's baby at the same time?"

"Is that the reason for the abortion?"

"Does Brooklyn know about this?" The questions came from all angles. Cameras flashed, reporters yelled over each other, and they all crowded around her.

When she finally made it to her Mercedes, Shonte' pressed the gas pedal as low as it could go and skirted out of the parking lot. She floored it like a lunatic all the way home, crying from the pain but more so from the burning shame of what she had just done.

When she arrived home, she depressingly dropped her Gucci bag at the front door. With her head low, tears in her eyes, and a snotty nose, she kicked off her Chanel sandals and walked towards the living room. To her surprise, Brooklyn was sitting on the couch watching the celebrity gossip channel.

"Babe, I didn't see your car," Shonte' said as she looked towards the front door and then back again at Brooklyn. She had a quizzical look on her face. She was completely perplexed by how he arrived at their mansion.

"Yeah, it's still at the airport. I grabbed a taxi. I started to get a little worried when you weren't answering your phone, but by the looks of it, I didn't have much to be worried about, did I?"

Shonte' glanced over at the oversized T.V. and saw the video of her walking out of the abortion clinic. "Wait! Babe, let me explain..."

He interrupted her. "You mean I'm out here working, and at the same time, you're killing my baby."

"Wait, Brooklyn, what about the show? You can't just disappoint your fans like that."

"Girl fuck that show. My baby is dead. Plus, we're doing a warm-up show right here in Brooklyn before we leave for Canada. But fuck all that right now."

"Babe, please just listen to me." Shonte' reached out to Brooklyn and grabbed his hand. She gently rubbed it as if trying to soothe his thoughts with her touch. "I.... I.... Well, you know, we just weren't ready and um... With your shows, tours, and scheduling, now just wasn't the right time. Baby, I love you, and I can't wait to have your baby, but right now, it just wasn't right." Shonte' moved in closer to Brooklyn as if she was going to hug him, but Brooklyn refused to allow it and pushed her so hard she fell to the floor banging her head against the wall in the hallway.

"Oh my God. Are you ok?" he asked. He walked over to her and wanted to touch her, but he couldn't bring himself to console her. He looked up and saw himself in the mirror; with his hand raised, he realized that he was on the verge of becoming violent with her and immediately calmed himself down.

Shonte' lay on the floor, bawling with tears and grief. She became louder. The bawling turned into boohooing and snot crying. "Oh God! I am so sorry. God, I am so sorry, Brooklyn." She crawled towards his feet.

He tried to walk away. "Get off of me, Shonte'. Let go now!" He shook his leg, but Shonte' was still attached. Brooklyn tried again to shake her, but Shonte's grip was tight. He continued strolling towards the door with Shonte' dragging behind him.

"Please, Brooklyn, just hear me out," she screeched.

He stopped temporarily and looked down at her with a look of pity and sorrow. "My seed, Shonte'? You killed Majesty? I can't believe you did that to me. I bought him a baseball mitt while I was on my way to the airport. My heart is broken in ways I can't even explain right now. Matter a fact, get the fuck out!"

"Brooklyn…" Shonte' pleaded with him.

He said it louder, "You better get the fuck out before I make you."

After fighting with herself to hold back the truth, Shonte' screamed and shouted, and the truth poured out of her like the air from a deflating balloon. "It wasn't yours." She repeated it several times with tears in her eyes and the voice of a record scratching. "It wasn't yours," she said, exhaling between the tears and hyperventilating.

"What?" By the look on Brooklyn's face, Shonte' knew she was in trouble. Brooklyn's eyebrow was raised and the vein was throbbing in his forehead. "Oh, so not only do you abort the son I thought I had, but you fucking somebody else too?" The look of disappointment and anguish made Shonte' feel like she had lost Brooklyn's love forever. His eyes were watery with tears, and his body was dropped with defeat. Shonte' could see his heart beating through his chest as his white T-Shirt rose and collapsed quickly.

"Bitch you must be trying to die today, you could've kept that shit to yourself."

Shonte' walked over to him, gasping between hiccups. "Please just listen to me, I'm not fucking nobody else. It was Ronny's"

Brooklyn stopped and took a deep breath. "The nigga that's locked up? The nigga that tried to kill me?"

"Yes... Please just let me explain."

"Please explain to me how a nigga in jail got you pregnant."

Shonte' tried to compose herself between sniffles. "Before you and I ever met, Ronny and I had a fling in college. It only happened once. A while back, he showed up at me and Michael's talking about Michael being his new agent. We all had dinner that night, and since he was in town, my boss asked me to do a story about him. I begged her to send someone else because I had already dreamed of having an affair with him, but my boss declined and threatened to fire me if I didn't show up. Ronny and I had sex at the stadium. During our moment of passion, someone recorded the entire thing and sent it to Michael."

"Oh, another recording of you huh? You are quite the celebrity, always getting caught red-handed. You are a piece of work."

Shonte' rolled her eyes, ignoring the sarcastic comment, and continued on with the story. "When I got home, Michael was furious. We argued, and he left. I was home alone for a few days until one night, while I was in the shower, Ronny snuck into our home and took a shower with me. Brooklyn, I swear I thought it was Michael."

"Wait a minute, you had no idea who you were fucking?"

"No, I didn't, it was dark, and he turned the lights out. Then he left before I got out of the shower. The night he tried to kill Michael, he mentioned something about me having his baby, but I didn't know what he was talking about until today. Baby, I'm sorry... I'm so sorry. But the baby wasn't yours."

"And what makes you know that for a fact? You have no idea who the father was, Shonte'. I'm about to do this show tonight. I will holla at you when I get back from Canada."

Brooklyn reached the front door with Shonte' still attached to his leg. He used all of this strength to pry her off of him, he had no more words for her. He looked at her one last time and a tear dropped from his hazel eyes. He shook his head in disgust, slammed the door, jumped on his Ducati motorcycle and sped out the driveway of their posh mansion toward the golden gates.

Shonte' just lay there near the front door of their empty, dark mansion, still sobbing and crying. Her clothes were wrinkled, half torn, and soaking wet with tears. Every sniffle, cough, and mumble echoed back as if even the walls were upset with her.

Shonte' stayed there all night, slumped over against the wall crying, wishing for her lover to return, but her cries would go unanswered. She knew in her heart she may have lost the love of her life forever.

*

Chapter 7: Canada

When Brooklyn's private jet landed at the airstrip in Canada, thousands of fans awaited his arrival. They were wearing all of their merch as well as their brightest smiles. They gathered in crowds and held posters and signs that read: Brooklyn Canada loves you. Brooklyn was amazed at how much love he was being shown in a different country.

"Man, I had no idea Canada had this much love for me."

Brooklyn exited the plane right into a media frenzy. Cameras and fans were everywhere. It took five bodyguards to get him from the plane to the car. Brooklyn signed a few autographs, hopped in the limo, and was delighted to hear the sound of the screeching tires as the tarmac met the rubber tires.

During the bumpy ride to the hotel, Brooklyn was silent, and thoughts of Shonte' whisked through his mind. He decided to send her a text. He reluctantly texted her to let her know the flight had landed and he had made it safely.

His screen lit up with a reply as soon as he hit send. He saw the message and all the feelings of disgust started to conjure up in his mind. He was so fired up with anger and disappointment that he turned the phone off and never bothered to reply.

Brooklyn sat in the limo alone and contemplated what was happening in his relationship with Shonte'. His emotions got the best of him, and a tear fell from his left eye. He couldn't help but think about how Shonte' had gone about things. He just kept thinking, what if the baby was mine? What if she aborted my baby? I can't believe she didn't even attempt to talk to me about this.

The Limo pulled up the swanky hotel and Brooklyn decided to put his depressing thoughts behind him. He put on his dark sunglasses and exited the limo. As he entered the golden doors, his eyes brightened and he couldn't hold back his expressions. "Got Damn! This shit is fucking dope," he exclaimed.

He walked into *Hotel Le St. James Montreal* and quickly realized he was in the company of extreme luxury. Brooklyn decided to look the hotel up on his phone and began to read the ratings. "Wow! Five stars, huh? Ok. I believe it."

He walked up to the concierge and said, "Hi I'm…"

"Oh my God! I know who you are," the young lady behind the desk said, cutting him short. "You're M.C. Brooklyn, right? Game Over is the dopest song I've ever heard."

Brooklyn's face turned red with embarrassment. "Oh, is it really?" he asked.

"Yes, it is," she said. "Can I get a quick picture with you Mr. Brooklyn? My Sister and I are big fans of your music. She would be so upset if I met you and didn't at least get a picture with you."

"Ok, sure. Why not?" he said. Brooklyn posed with the fan and threw up two fingers that represented peace.

"Thank you so much Brooklyn, and since you were so nice to take a picture with me, I am going to comp your room. You don't have to pay for anything. Here is your keycard. The bellhop will help you with your bags."

"Um… Ok. Are you sure you can do that? I don't want to get you in trouble."

"No it's cool, my father owns the building," she said.

"Oh, in that case, right on! Thanks again." Brooklyn strolled over to the bellhop, smiling from ear to ear. "I guess there are a few perks to this fame thing," he said.

"I'll take your bags Mr. Brooklyn," the bellhop said, and escorted Brooklyn to the shiny golden-mirrored elevators.

Brooklyn was obsessed with room number 227 and would only ever stay in that room no matter what hotel he was in. Brooklyn entered the room and kissed the locket that was around his neck. "I told you, no matter where I go, you will always be with me."

2-2-7 was the birthday of his stillborn first child. Brooklyn vowed that no matter where he stayed he would always be in room 227 in remembrance of his firstborn.

The bellhop left Brooklyn's bags in his room and received a hefty one-hundred-dollar tip for his services. "Thank you, my good sir," Brooklyn said with a smirk.

This wasn't Brooklyn's first time in luxury, so he wasn't completely astonished. However, he was impressed. "Man! I wouldn't mind staying in my room the entire trip." He walked over to the Balcony. "I love you Canada," he yelled.

A few fans still waiting outside yelled back, "We love you too Brooklyn!"

Brooklyn stood on the balcony with his arms crossed and his head tilted and thought, now this is the life. He walked back into the glamorous hotel and admired the greatness before him. He picked up a wine glass, and it sparkled back at him. The sun bounced in and out of the room like a zigzag, and the view of the city made Brooklyn smile with excitement.

The Tempur-Pedic bed was calling Brooklyn's name. He fell face first on the bed and closed his eyes to get some much-needed rest.

Just as he drifted off, it was clear now- God himself was at his door, throwing thunder like fists, each clap slamming against the wood like He was fed up.

Brooklyn jolted upright, widened his eyes and reached to his side for the weapon he always carried in the hip-holster at his side. "Who is it?" he yelled.

"Yo Brook, we got some hotties out here and a bottle of that Ace, you in?"

Brooklyn peeped out the peephole and said, "Nah I'm good. Y'all go ahead, Imma chill tonight," he replied in a groggy voice.

"Aight then. Just means more for me."

Brooklyn plopped back down on the Tempur-Pedic bed again, hoping to get some much-needed rest. I just need ten minutes, he thought. Yeah. Ten minutes and I'm good. Brooklyn turned his phone back on to set the alarm. He set the alarm to wake him up right before it was time for the show, and closed his eyes.

Just as he did, his phone started to go off as if it were purposely trying to wake him up. Brooklyn's phone vibrated so much that it fell off the nightstand and onto the floor. "Damn! Can't a nigga get a minute to sleep? Shit."

Brooklyn picked up the phone and looked at the screen to see what all the fuss was about. "Thirty missed calls?" he exclaimed. What the fuck is wrong with Shonte' – what the fuck? Got damn, who the fuck calls somebody thirty muthafuckin times?

This shit is ridiculous, and it's gotta be stopped, he thought. This girl is outta control, and what the fuck are all these text messages about?

One thread of messages read:

Baby please can we talk about this? I want to fix this. Please don't be mad at me anymore. I will do anything. Just tell me and I will do it.

Hello???

Brooklyn WTF? We need to talk please call me?

Ok. I see you are ignoring me. You are going way too far with this Brooklyn. Please call me as soon as possible.

Ok. Now I'm starting to get pissed the fuck off. I can't believe you're not even going to respond to my messages. The last thing we need is to be apart from each other right now. Our love is deeper than that Brooklyn. I will do anything for you. If you do not respond to my messages I will find out where you are staying and I will find you Brooklyn!!!

Brooklyn's anger grew with each message he read. He decided at this point she needed to hear his voice. The speaker on his phone only managed to spit out one ring before she answered. "A.... A...Yo...Let me explain one muthfuckin thing to you. I'm a grown man. What you not gone do is tell me when, where and how I'm supposed to fucking act.

"But…" Shonte' tried to interject.

"No! shut the fuck up right now Shonte'. I'm talking and after the stunt you just pulled I shouldn't even be having no conversation with you at all, but I love you girl and this shit is real. I aint no punk ass nigga and I know you aint used to dealing with a real one so let me teach you."

"Brooklyn!" Shonte' yelled.

"Didn't I tell you to hold the fuck up and let me speak?"

Shonte' was in tears, but the growl and command in his voice muted her immediately. She was getting aroused.

"Look, Imma holla at you when I holla at you. Give me some space, and when I'm ready to discuss this bullshit, I will get at you," he said. "Aight?"

"Ok," she replied.

They both hung up the phones – Shonte' crying on one end of the line; Brooklyn cursing her on the other.

"Fuck!" Brooklyn threw his phone at the wall, and it shattered the screen. He plopped back down on the bed, hoping to get some shuteye, but thoughts of Shonte' continued in his mind. Shit, I can't fucking sleep. He grabbed his shattered phone and called a good friend and label mate.

"Hello?" the sexy voice on the other end said.

"Hello. Do you know who this is?" Brooklyn asked.

"Of course, I know who this is. How are you, Brooklyn?"

"I'm good… I'm good. Out here in cold-ass, Canada doing a show."

"Get outta here! Me too!"

"Then we need to link up. When can you come through?"

"Let me just figure out my schedule. Can I call you back?" she asked.

"Yeah, Aight! Holla at you later."

They both hung up and couldn't help but think about what it would be like if they finally saw each other again.

*

Brooklyn was getting ready for his show that night, trying on outfits and checking himself out in the tall mirror built into the wardrobe. He stopped momentarily, sat on the edge of the bed, and thought, *Man, I don't even wanna do this shit tonight.* He looked at Shonte's picture on his phone and rubbed the image as if he was rubbing her forehead.

I just wanted us to be happy forever. I was even going to propose to you, girl. You have no idea what you've just done. His face was blemished with sadness.

Brooklyn picked up a glass and poured himself a shot of Louis the Thirteenth that was neatly placed next to his bedside. He slammed the glass down on the nightstand, looked in the mirror and said, "Aight, let's do this shit."

He walked out of the hotel room, into the elevator, and into the lobby, where his bodyguards were awaiting his arrival. "You ready, Brook?" the largest one asked.

"Yeah, let's go, G!" Brooklyn put on his Versace shades and exited the lobby with his entourage. Fans were still outside yelling and screaming his name. "We love you, M.C. Brooklyn!" they shouted. "I love you too," he yelled back.

Brooklyn hopped into the limo and talked with his entourage the entire ride. They laughed about the women they had been with and the money they had made. The trip was short and when they arrived at the stadium, Brooklyn's heart still wasn't in the show. He climbed out of the limo with his head down, staring at the sidewalk.

"Yo Brook, you alright, bro?" his bodyguard asked.

"Yeah. Yeah, I'm good," he replied.

His entourage whisked him from the limo, through the building and straight into the backstage area. The crowd was screaming and yelling for him. "M.C. Brooklyn! We want Brooklyn!"

Brooklyn peeked out through the curtain and saw a sea of people with M.C Brooklyn signs that read the title of his new single. "Yall see this shit?" Brooklyn asked. "This shit is crazy."

Monster joined him at the curtain. "I see it bro, those muthafuckas are thirsty tonight," he said.

"There's one bitch out there with a T-Shirt on that says, Brooklyn I will fuck you for free! Damn, they love me more in Canada than in the U.S.A. I just might have to move here," he said with a smile. Brooklyn closed the curtain and started to prepare for his entrance on stage.

The curtains slid open, and Brooklyn just stood there frozen. The crowd became quiet. Brooklyn gazed across the sea of people, and suddenly, it all came back to him. He yelled into the Microphone, "Does Canada love M.C. Brooklyn?"

"Yes!" the crowd yelled back.

"I don't think ya'll heard me. Does Canada love Brooklyn?" "Hell

Yeah!" the crowd yelled back. Brooklyn ran across the

stage like an animal. He was back in his element, and nothing could faze him now. That night, Brooklyn gave Canada the performance of a lifetime.

When it came time to close the show, he said, "RIP Lyric and Majesty. One Love!" And then the curtains closed. Brooklyn was quickly whisked into his limo and escorted to his hotel.

*

Brooklyn entered his hotel room and crashed on his plush mattress in hopes of getting a good night's rest again.

About ten seconds later, the beautiful picture of one of Canada's great lakes fell off of the wall, because the knocks hit so hard, it felt like Mike Tyson was out there, pounding the door like it owed him money. "Yeah?" Brooklyn mumbled, but no one heard him. The knock just got louder and harder.

Brooklyn jumped up and made his way to the door.

"Man, I told you, I ain't fuckin wit ya'll." He angrily swung open the door without even looking through the peephole. "Man, I told y'all..." He stopped mid-sentence and was at a loss for words. Still stunned, he muttered, "Wow, I wasn't expecting you until later."

Kali was standing there with one foot stepped in front of her and her body slanted as if she were posing for a men's magazine. With a devious smile, she said, "Of course, you weren't, that's what makes it a surprise. Now are you going to invite me in or are we just gonna stand here and stare at each other all night?"

Kali was a black goddess. Dark smooth skin that looked like someone had baked dark chocolate in the oven and melted it onto her. Her hair was naturally long and jet black. She had the natural shape of an African woman, gifted with the perfect hips and thighs and a twenty-four-inch waist. Kali was the type of woman men across the globe fantasized about, and yet here she was, standing in the hallway of Brooklyn's Hotel.

"Of course not. Come on in." Brooklyn stepped to the side and watched her as she passed him. She was wearing a tan trench coat, and – judging by the way it was tightly hugging her curvaceous figure – very little else.

"Wow Brooklyn, this room is as big as my studio apartment in L.A. This is beautiful. Why aren't you sharing it with the infamous Shonte'?"

Brooklyn acted like he didn't hear a word she said. "Would you like a drink?"

"Nah I'm good, been clean for a while now. Don't wanna go back down that road again. So, what's up Brooklyn?" Kali started to unbutton her trench coat. Her lips were glossy and she licked them slowly and deliberately.

Brooklyn watched her as he stood there in his bathrobe. He wanted to say her name but his throat wouldn't let him.

"You seem a little tense. Is there anything I can do to relieve you?" She continued her striptease.

Brooklyn poured a shot and just watched her every move. Kali moved her body like a goddess. She was slow and intentional with every sway of her hips. She was wearing a purple thong and a matching purple bra that accentuated her double-D breasts like they were sitting on a throne.

"I see you're wearing my favorite color," he said.

"Now, you didn't think I forgot, did you?" Kali stepped closer to Brooklyn, shoving him backward into the armchair behind him. She knelt in front of him, untied his bathrobe, and massaged his genitals until he was all the way erect.

She took her time with him, placing kisses everywhere she knew would drive him crazy. Brooklyn's legs and body were shaking uncontrollably. Once Kali knew she had him right where she wanted him, she continued to tease him, and right before she put it in her mouth, she licked it soft and succulently until it was wet.

Brooklyn slurred his speech. "Shit… Got Damn girl! Oh my God! What the fuck are you doing to me?"

She stopped and softly blew her warm breath over every part of him. Kali was the only one that could bring out Brooklyn's milky substance strictly by licking and sucking him. She knew what he wanted and always knew exactly what to do.

Brooklyn ejaculated in her mouth, and she loved every minute of it. She smiled once he was done, kissed him, and lay down on the bed. Brooklyn showered and joined her.

"Brooklyn, you didn't ask me over here just for some head. So, you gonna talk to me or do you wanna just handle it alone?"

Brooklyn was smoking a cigar. He looked at her and told her exactly what was wrong. "Shonte' had an abortion."

"What? She aborted your baby?" Kali scrunched her eyebrows in disappointment and disbelief.

"Yeah. I had a name picked out and everything. I was gonna call him Majesty." Brooklyn's eyebrows were raised and his face lit up with hopeless excitement when he said Majesty's name.

"What the fuck is wrong with her? See, I used to like her, but now she got a problem with me," she said, rolling her eyes and neck.

"Kali, you and I go way back – since middle school. I will always have a special place in my heart for you, and I appreciate you so much. I wish it could have worked out."

"Yeah me too but that was your call. I will always love you Brooklyn, but you still hold me accountable for something I didn't do. I just cleaned myself up and got sober for the guilt I've been carrying."

"Kali… Now you're playing the victim."

"Brooklyn, you don't think that shit hurt me too? You don't think I cried for years behind that shit? But the fact is, it wasn't my fault, and I am done letting you blame me for it. You left me there alone to process all that shit by myself. When our daughter was stillborn, it devastated me too. Brooklyn, you are not the only one with feelings."

"Yeah, baby, I know, and I am so sorry. I was nineteen then, and I'm twenty-four now. I understand I was wrong, and I should have been there for you. I'm sorry. I can't fix the past, but I can try to make it right. Will you let me do that?" He stroked her neck as he spoke.

"Yes, I will. I can't believe Shonte' had an abortion. Here I am, dying to have your baby, and she effortlessly kills hers. Life can be so fucked up."

"Well, she said it might not have been mine."

"Got Damn! How many people is she fucking? Brooklyn, are you sure this is the chick you wanna be with?" Kali pulled back slightly, displaying her shock.

"I know, but I love her; shouldn't that be all that matters?" It even sounded naïve to him.

"No, it shouldn't. You should never marry for love and love only. I mean, love can be there, but there has to be so much more."

"So much more like what?"

"Like this. Like us right here," she said as she stared into his soul.

Brooklyn nodded and kissed Kali on her glossy lips, moving slowly onto her neck. He bit it hard and whispered in her ear. "Yeah you like that, huh? Now, don't think I forgot either. I can't and will never forget you or what we've been through together." He picked Kali up.

Her legs were wrapped around his waist, and he walked them over to the wide-open balcony.

He looked out at the pitch-black city as he made love to Kali slow and rough, just how she liked it. She moaned quietly and gently rubbed her hands over his brown body. "I miss you," Kali said while he thrust into her.

Brooklyn looked into her eyes and said, "I love you." He gave her several meaningful thrusts. Brooklyn was making love to Kali like this was the last time he would ever see her again. Their connection was like the meeting of two souls that were destined to be one. From the balcony to the table, their bodies were joined, their souls were connected, and for a short time, it felt like their souls had left the earth, and together, they were soaring beyond the planet.

When their souls found their way back to earth, Brooklyn was on top of Kali, and they were lying on the bed. Brooklyn gave Kali one last long and slow thrust and left his juices inside of her. His body fell on top of her. He grabbed her like she was the last person on earth; Kali hugged him back.

They lay in each other's arms for the rest of the night, their hearts beating in unison.

*

The next morning, Brooklyn woke while Kali was still sleeping. He turned on his iPhone and noticed there was a message from Shonte'. He turned it back off and instead looked at Kali as she slept like an angel. He got up, got dressed and headed to his bodyguard's room.

He banged on the door several times before Big Psycho answered. It was a name only fit for a man who could crush skulls with his bare hands. Big Psycho had done that more times than he had eaten hot meals.

"Damn, finally," Brooklyn said as he passed Psycho. "Look man, I need to call a jeweler. Can you get in contact with some people? I need a diamond. An engagement ring."

"Damn, you finally about to propose to Shonte'?"

"Man, stop asking me questions and answer me. Do you know one or not? You are all in my business like you, the police bro."

"I don't know one but I can get one for you. All I gotta do is drop your name, and they will call like crazy." He smiled at that,

120

proud that he got to work for M.C. Brooklyn. "All I gotta say is Brooklyn needs a diamond, and my phone will be buzzing like crazy. Rich ass, buying diamonds just for the fuck of it," he said.

"Fuck you, man," Brooklyn said with a smile. "Ok, you do that for me. Thanks."

As Psycho made a few phone calls, Brooklyn stood near the window watching people move throughout the city. "Man Psyche… Have you ever paid attention to how this shit looks, just like the Matrix? I mean people coming and going because they are told to. Everyone is moving in sequence. I can't live like that."

"Ok," he replied. Here we go with this man on the moon talk. Look, the jeweler is on his way. I managed to get one of your favorites."

"Oh yeah? Who?"

"Jacoby. He said he happened to be in the area."

"Yeah, right. I swear that dude be following me sometimes."

*

Jacoby arrived right on time, wearing a cheap suit and fine gold jewelry. "Mr. Brooklyn, good to see you again."

"Yeah, ok, Jacoby, skip the small talk. What you got for me?"

"Only my most prized diamonds for you, Mr. Brooklyn. Now what is it that you are looking for? Is it a new chain, I have platinum and gold?"

"Nah, J, it's for a lady. I need an engagement ring. Something never-before-seen. Do you have a black diamond?"

"Oh yes, Mr. Brooklyn, I have something special for you." Jacoby pulled out another roll of jet-black diamonds. As soon as Brooklyn saw it he knew it was the one.

The ring was black with platinum trim and a black diamond that sat on top of a platinum crown. It was the most unique and beautiful ring Brooklyn had ever laid eyes on. The rock was ten carats flaw- less; so large it almost didn't look real.

"That's it. That's the one," Brooklyn said.

"Ah Mr. Brooklyn, I figured you would like that. I happen to have a matching band for you as well. Can I interest you in a necklace for the lady?"

"Nah I'm good, just the diamonds."

"Ok, suit yourself, but they're gonna sell out. I hear Gaga's in town, and you know she loves her diamonds." Jacoby let his eyes linger in Brooklyn's direction, as if he was trying to tempt him through nothing more than his gaze.

Brooklyn shook his head. "No J, that will be all." He gave him his black card.

Jacoby swiped it on his phone. "Thank You Mr. Brooklyn, it's a pleasure doing business with you."

"Hey before you leave, how much did you just run my card for?"

"Just a small eighty-five thousand. I gave you a discount since we always do business together. Enjoy your tour, Mr. Brooklyn. How long will you be staying?"

"I don't know Jacoby. I might just have to move here," he said.

Brooklyn cracked a slight smile at the very thought of her wearing his wedding ring and being called Mrs. Miller. The excitement was overtaking him, and he couldn't wait much longer.

He left the room and made his way back to room 227, where Kali was waiting right where he had left her.

Brooklyn and Kali had known each other for years. Their talents brought them together when they did a duo for their middle school talent show. Kali sang her way to the hearts of the audience, and Brooklyn won them over with his growling voice. When Brooklyn signed his first contract, he made sure Kali had one too. He had lived his life knowing that she would have done the exact same thing for him.

When Brooklyn entered the bedroom, Kali was still sleeping like a beautiful black Angel. Brooklyn slapped her on her naked ass and said, "Wake up, there's something I need to ask you."

*

Chapter 8: New York New York

Her mood was a notch above rock bottom today. Not by much, though—just barely off the floor. The past two days had her spirit dragging so low even hope had stopped trying to lift it. Shonte' tried to keep herself busy with work by writing a few columns here and there. She wanted to give Brooklyn his space, but she also knew too much space could end their relationship. After Brooklyn told her he would get back to her, she honored his request, but that didn't stop her from losing her mind.

Shonte' was startled from her day dream of Brooklyn as the echoing thuds burst the silence like a gunshot in the night. "What the fuck is that?" Shonte' was taken from her fantasy of reconciling with Brooklyn and brought back to reality.

"Open the door!" the voice on the other side of it shouted.

Shonte' crept around their mansion, trying to figure out what they were doing here again. She snuck a peak out the back window and saw the property crawling with undercover cops.

I'm not answering the door, she thought. If they want to come in they will have to make their way in.

The knocking echoed again, only louder this time, because that was somehow possible. "Ok," a voice shouted, "we will be back with a warrant since you want to play games, Brooklyn." The police seemed to leave in a hurry, but Shonte' knew they were probably still camped out somewhere close.

She frantically placed a call to Brooklyn. The voicemail came on the first ring. She called back several times, and each time, she got voicemail. "Fuck," she exclaimed angrily. "I fucking hate when he does this shit! This is so crazy."

Shonte' ran upstairs to their exquisite bedroom and grabbed a few items of his clothing. She picked out eight of his favorite pairs of clothing, grabbed the scissors and for each time he ignored her phone call, she cut a hole in the middle of his pants. "Let's see how he likes this when he gets home," Shonte' said devilishly. "If he wants crazy, his sorry ass just got it."

The phone rang and interrupted her devious plot. "Brooklyn!" she exclaimed.

"Wait a minute before you start yelling. Calm yourself down. I already told you I ain't trying to hear the bullshit. So, what the fuck you want anyway?" he asked.

"What the fuck do I want? Ok. I'm going to ignore that and just chop it up to your feelings being hurt. I already apologized and I can't do anything more than that."

"Actually, there's a whole lot more you can do and should have done, but we are past all that. What are you calling me for?" Kali snarled at him while he was on the phone with Shonte, but she knew not to say a word.

"The police were just here again," she replied.

"Ok. So, what did you tell them?"

"Nothing, I didn't answer. But they said they would be back with a warrant."

"Ok. Then you already know what to do," he replied sarcastically.

"Brooklyn, is there something you need to tell me?"

"Shonte', you know everything you need to know. Why are you asking me this anyway? Are you working for them now?"

"Brooklyn, you know I would never do anything like that. I love you way too much."

"Then you just keep doing what you been doing and we won't have any problems. Aight?" he said.

"Can you at least tell me how long the tour is and how long you will be gone?

"No, I can't but I will get at you when I'm ready. Peace." Brooklyn hung up the phone and ended the conversation.

Shonte' went back to cutting up his clothes and cursing his name. Recently, communicating with Brooklyn had been getting extremely difficult and Shonte' started to wonder what was really going on with him. She didn't want to read too much into it because she was still living in their mansion and Brooklyn continued to take care of her financially. There was always money wired to her bank account, the bills were paid, and sometimes he would even send her extra for a new bag or a pair of shoes.

But trying to talk to Brooklyn was like pulling teeth and it was getting to be a bit much for her. Even though she was used to him being away for long periods of time, this time, it was different, and she could feel it in her bones.

That was it. The moment it happened. A thunderous boom ripped through the mansion like a warhead had dropped dead center. If the meteor that killed the dinosaurs had a modern-day relative, it had just smashed into her living room—and it didn't come alone. "What the fuck!?" Shonte' screamed. "What the hell was that?" She stood at the top of the stairs wearing only a T-Shirt and panties, with a .44 magnum handgun with it pointed straight at the intruders.

"Put the gun down, young lady; we're not going to hurt you," one of the detectives said. He pulled out a piece of paper that he claimed was a warrant.

Shonte' put the gun down, went inside her bedroom, and put on a pair of sweatpants. The officers trailed quickly behind her. She sat on the bed while they ransacked the entire home.

The officer served her with the warrant and said, "Nice home you've got here, miss; where's your boyfriend?"

"Fuck you," she said.

"Ok. I see you want to make this difficult. How would you like it if I took you down to the station? I bet your boyfriend would pop up then, wouldn't he?"

"You can't touch me, pig! Put your hands on me, and I will make sure you, your kids, and your grandkids never work in this jurisdiction ever again!" She collected her thoughts for a moment, cooling them so they weren't so rash and flaming. "Brooklyn's on tour, but if you're any kind of real investigator, shouldn't you know that already? Why do ya'll ask questions that you already have the answers to? Your warrant is to search the house, not to search me or ask me any kind of questions. From now on, you have your conversations with this house, and don't say another word to me." Shonte' rolled her eyes.

She jogged downstairs, where the eighty-inch T.V. played one of Brooklyn's videos. "Oh yeah, there he is... Why don't you go get him?" Shonte' shouted to the detective, who was still standing at the top of the gallery stairs. She turned the video as loud as possible and plopped down on the Italian leather couch.

"Oh, you think you're pretty funny, huh?" the officer said as he entered the room. "You think you're untouchable because your boyfriend's rich." Once he got close enough, he softly said, "Don't you know I can take you in on conspiracy charges for aiding and abetting a criminal? Shonte', I want you to think long, hard, and clear about what you are doing."

Shonte' heard glass shattering as the officers were deliberately tearing apart their multi-million-dollar mansion. "You just gonna let them tear up the whole fucking house?" she asked the detective.

"Well," he said with his eyebrows raised, "you could always tell us what we need to know and we will be out of your hair forever."

"Fuck you," Shonte' exclaimed and spat in the officer's face. "Why, you fucking little cunt bitch!" The detective raised his hand to hit her; Shonte' turned her face, preparing for the blow.

Right then, an officer reached out, grabbed the detective's hand, and said, "She's not worth it." He pulled the detective back. "It's time to go; we didn't find anything anyway."

The detective took his handkerchief out of his pocket, wiped the spit from his face, and said, "Ok, you and your boyfriend may have gotten away this time, but one day, you won't be so lucky."

As the lead detective was making his way by her to walk out the door, he half-spun and gave her a smile that looked as though it was fresh from the deepest depths of Sarcasm Town. "I know your boyfriend had something to do with that incident in Philly, and he will get caught, and I will make him pay. I always get my guy. So, tell MC Brooklyn, Lance, or whatever he's calling himself these days that I am watching his every move. As soon as he slips up, I'm gonna be right there to catch him. Here's my card. Have a nice day."

Shonte' watched him in disgust and whispered, "Fucking ass-hole."

"Come on, boys, let's go. I think that's enough for today." The officers packed up their belongings and exited the lofty mansion. Shonte' wanted to slam the door, but it was hanging off the hinges from the battering ram. Angrily, she closed it as tight as she could.

*

The next day, Shonte' decided she wouldn't let her issues with Brooklyn, Ronny, and the police take control of her life. She called her best friend Mo.

"Hey girl, what are you doing?"

"Nothing much. Why, what's up?"

"I was thinking about going to that spa you've been raving so much about."

"Oh, not you... Not miss I'm-too-good-for-that-kind-of-thing. Are you sure you ready for all of that?"

"Yeah, girl, I need a break. This is getting way out of hand. I mean, between the shit with Brooklyn, Ronny, and the police, I just can't. I need to get away."

"Ok. Don't chicken out on me at the last minute, Shonte'. It's not easy getting into these kinds of places, and my name means something. So, don't fuck up."

"Ok. Ok. I won't. You have my word"

"Alright, I'm on my way, see you in a few."

Shonte' was excited. Mo had bragged so much to her about this new spa and she knew it was just what she needed.

Mo arrived right on time.

"Hey, fly girl," Shonte' said. Mo was in her drop-top convertible Bentley and wearing a white sundress with a matching scarf accentuating her beautiful ebony skin tone.

"How are you, miss Shonte'?" Mo said with a sarcastic smile. "Oh my God, Mo, I have so much to fill you in on." Shonte' got in the car. During the drive, Shonte' began to fill Mo in on all the gory details of what had become her life.

"Mo it's crazy. Brooklyn and I don't even speak anymore. I don't know if it's someone else or if he's still angry with me. I mean I know he's on tour but he used call, text or facetime. Now things are so different and I have no idea what to do."

"What? Shonte', are you kidding me? You haven't heard from him at all?"

"I mean we've spoken a few times but it's angry calls and he doesn't listen to me anymore. He cuts me off mid-sentence and doesn't even allow me to speak. I mean I know he's upset about this abortion and I want to give him some space, but this is ridiculous. Plus, everything reminds me of him. I hate this feeling."

Just then Brooklyn's song comes on the radio. The melody came blaring from the speakers as if Brooklyn had set this moment up himself.

"See that's exactly what I'm talking about."

Mo reached in and turned it off. "Shonte', Imma tell you like my mama told me. The more time a man spends away from you the further you guys are going to drift apart. I understand this was serious and he's very upset with you, but he needs to be upset around you, not away from you. Shit he probably has another girlfriend already. Shon- te' if you don't get your ass out there soon, you gonna be kissing your man goodbye."

"I never thought about it like that."

"Well you should. If you leave a man alone for too long they start to rely on their own thinking, and the last thing you want is him thinking for himself. You should have talked to him before you made that decision. You can try to fix it or deal with the broken pieces. But now let's get in the spa. I am super stressed, and this was perfect timing for me."

"What can I say girl? I guess my psyche just connected with yours and sensed that you were going through some shit too."

"You know what Shonte', sometimes I wonder if that's all that life is."

"And what would that be?"

"Just a constant cycle of going through shit. I'm telling you God has got to be a woman, because this shit right here that we be going through feels like a bitch that got her heart broken and is bitter as fuck."

Shonte' giggled. "Shut up you fool."

"You think I'm playing, shit I am serious as a heart attack honey."

Shonte' and Mo arrived at the spa, valet parked the Bentley and cheerfully made their way inside the spa. They were so elated they were practically skipping.

"I have a reservation for Monique and Shonte'."

"Yes ma'am right this way"

The hostess escorted them both to the waiting area and just as soon as they were seated, their names were called. They each got to choose their own masseuse, and they were just as handsome as the brochure said they were.

Monique had chosen a dark chocolate, six feet, abs-of-steel Jamaican with dreads. Shonte' opted for the brown-skinned, muscle-bound, tattooed type.

Shonte' flirted with him as he escorted her to the back room. This was not just any spa. This place specialized in providing orgasms to women strictly using their hands. When Shonte' entered the room, it was set up just like any ordinary spa. The only difference here was that their hands would be going much further than the small of her back. It helped that her masseuse was also very attractive.

"Ms. Smith, are you ready for your massage?" the masseuse asked.

"You have no idea how much I need this," Shonte' replied with a flirty smile.

"Well I am glad I'm the one who gets to bring you pleasure today."

"So am I. What's your name?"

"Keenen, but everyone calls me the Kure."

"And why is that?"

"I can show you better than I can tell you. Will you let me show you?"

Shonte' inched in closer and softly said, "Well the Kure, I have this tingling sensation that's throbbing between my legs. It keeps me up all hours of the night and it just won't stop. Do you have the antidote?"

"Baby I'm more than the antidote I'm the Kure to any and all ailments. By the time I'm done with you, you will have forgotten all of the problems you brought here today."

"Ok then, what are we waiting for? Let's get started"

Keenen escorted Shonte' to the massage table and began to work his magic. During the massage, all Shonte' could talk about was Brooklyn.

She lay on her stomach while the masseuse rubbed his special oil over her back and buttocks. He squeezed her cheeks gently and touched them lightly with his fingers. Shonte' paused in her conversa- tion about Brooklyn temporarily and focused on the warm sensations that were penetrating her body.

"Oh my," she said. "You have a way with your hands."

Keenan smiled but didn't say a word

Shonte' mentioned Brooklyn's name again. Keenen aggressively rubbed her bottom as if he was trying to punish her for mentioning his name.

"Oh shit! I like that. Harder," she said. Keenen complied with her command. "Oh Keenan! Your touch is amazing. You're doing things to my body that I have never experienced before." Keenan smacked her bottom hard. She let out a light scream like she was be- ing spanked for the first time in her life.

He continued on to her thighs, legs and feet. Shonte' was getting moist from his sensual touch. And right about now, she felt as though she needed a distraction. From life just as much as from the feeling in her lower half.

"What would you do if your girlfriend had aborted her baby without telling you because she wasn't sure if it was yours or not?"

He stopped massaging for a moment and whispered in her ear. "Miss Shonte', today we don't discuss our problems. Today, imagine that we are not even here on planet earth." He turned on the radio that played a Zen-like tone.

Shonte' breathed in deeply, closed her eyes and delved into the unknown of the moment. His hands, slippery from the oils, made their way down to her muscular buttocks and all the way up to her neck.

His hands were slippery and freely made their way all over her body. Shonte' couldn't help but moan with every sensation.

"Oh my God! My body is so hot, I'm shaking. Oh my God! I feel like I'm going to come. Oh my God. I can't believe this."

He took the tips of his fingers and waved them all over her body. He teased her by getting as close to her vagina as possible without actually inserting his hand at all.

Shonte''s body was already quivering and shaking uncontrollably. "Yes! Right there! Yes! Please don't stop."

He flipped Shonte' over and began to massage her breasts softly but with a fast motion. Her body began to tingle and she began breathing heavily. He slowed and worked his way down to her hips and thighs, still teasing her by getting as close to her privates as pos- sible without actually touching them.

Shonte's hips and lower body were moving around and around, in circles then up and down as if he was magically calling her body with his mind.

"What are you doing to me? I can't...I can't." Shonte's muscles were getting tighter and tighter, she was breathing heavily and her skin was so hot you could melt an iceberg on it. Shonte's legs locked up and she felt her vagina contracting with pure pleasure. The juices flowing from her body spewed out waterfall. He grabbed her body firmly and held her tightly against him until her body was completely done pulsating.

"Will that be all Miss Shonte', or can I interest you in a double?" he asked. With the severity of the nonchalance in his voice, you'd think he was asking her about the weather. It was as if he was blissful- ly unaware of the miracle he had just conducted.

"No, that will be all, thank you." Shonte' lay there for another ten minutes then got up, showered and left a one-hundred-dollar tip for her masseuse.

As Shonte' made her way out of the room, she could hardly walk and her legs felt like rubber. This was her first experience, but it was one of several for Monique, and she didn't seem fazed at all. "How was your first massage?" Monique asked with a sly look on her face.

"Jeez Monique, how come you didn't tell me it was this intense? I feel like I am floating on a cloud."

"If I had told you how great it was you would have thought I was exaggerating. I see you had the Kure." Monique winked her eye at Shonte'.

"Yes, I did, and boy am I cured, if you catch my drift. How was your massage?"

"Girl, you know I don't kiss and tell. Let's just say my massage turned into dual pleasure."

"Mo! You're an animal," Shonte' said.

"What can I say, Shonte'? I always try my best." They both laughed.

"Thanks again Mo. You are always there when I need you."

"That's what girls do for each other. You better just make sure you find Brooklyn's ass before some other bitch does."

"You think I should just go out there?" Shonte' asked. "Do you think that's what it takes to get your man back?"

"Mo, I don't know. He's very angry with me and the last thing I want is to piss him off even more." Shonte's unsureness was apparent in her voice.

"What's the worst that could happen? He's already mad at you and I can't see him getting more upset than he already is. At least if you go you will have the answers you need, and you can move on or you can stay and wait for him. The choice is yours, but you better hur- ry up and make it. Men like Brooklyn have women throwing themselves at them, and a man is just a man Shonte'. They get vulner- able just like we do."

"I don't know, I guess you're right. I'll think about it." And Shonte' did have to think about it, way more than she ever knew.

*

Chapter 9: Killa Kali

Back in Canada, spirits were higher than ever.

Brooklyn knelt down on one knee near the bed Kali was lying on, the ring in hand nestled between his index finger and thumb. Kali was jumping up and down like she had just won the lottery.

"Oh my God Brooklyn... You're not... Oh my God." Kali raised her hand to her mouth, trying to hold back the excitement, but she couldn't. She blurted out and said yes before Brooklyn could even ask the question.

"Hold on baby... Let me do this, ok?"

"Ok," she said nervously.

The butler entered the room playing the violin version of R. Kelly's top hit song I Wanna Marry the Pussy. The bellhop had a bottle of champagne sitting on ice, waiting to be uncorked at the perfect moment.

"Baby, I know this is sudden, but when I'm with you the pain disappears. You make me happy and I want to be with you forever. I don't remember ever feeling like this. You bring me up when I am down, you make me feel like a king in a world of mediocrity and the sex...well let's just say it's fucking explosive. Out of all the women that I have been with, I have to say you bring me the most joy. Will you marry me?" He slid the ring onto her finger.

"Yes Brooklyn, yes. Yes, I will marry you!" She jumped on him and kissed his face so hard she knocked him down to the floor.

The bellhop popped the champagne and Brooklyn signaled for them to go. Kali was ripping his clothes off him the second the door closed behind them, but he grabbed her hand and said, "I gotta tell you something. I haven't officially broken it off with Shonte', so can you keep this on the D-L until I get a chance to talk to her?"

"Yeah whatever, with a ring this big it will buy you a few weeks. But you better hurry up and get that shit done. I'm not trying to be no third wheel."

Brooklyn turned on his iPhone to let Shonte' know he would fly home next week to talk to her, but before he could reach the text message thread, the notification for her voicemail popped up. He pressed the phone to his ear and awaited his fate. "Fuck," he yelled.

"What?" Kali asked. "Shonte's on her way here, she left me a message. That was about an hour ago. It only takes an hour and twenty minutes to get from New York to here." Brooklyn was wrestling with his clothes, trying to put them on quickly. He threw Kali's clothes at her as he moved. "Get dressed, we gotta get going."

"Why are you in such a rush? Now you can tell her in person. That makes it easier for us to be together."

"Kali, you know it's never that simple. She is still staying in my house and all my shit is there. You know if she finds out about this muthafucka is as good as gone. I got a lot of expensive shit in that house. Kali, you can't be here when she comes. I will get you another room at another hotel; you just gotta go, now."

"Wait a minute. Five seconds ago you were proposing to me, now you are throwing me out of your room? No chance. I will take another room but I want one in this hotel."

"Ok fine, whatever. Go downstairs, get the room and tell them to charge it to me."

"Ok, but you better tell her. And I mean soon." She kissed him softly on his lips and grabbed his dick on the way out.

Kali followed Brooklyn's instructions and went directly to the front desk to get another room. As she waited, she continued to ad- mire the rock Brooklyn had just placed on her hand. She smiled as the diamond blinged each way she turned her hand.

"Wow I still can't believe he proposed," she said out loud.

"Next", the woman's voice startled Kali from her admiration and she swiftly walked up to the counter.

"Hi I need a room please, and can you charge it to Brooklyn."

"Ok ma'am, I just need to step away for a moment to confirm with Mr. Brooklyn. Will it be ok if I step away for a moment to place a phone call?"

"Sure."

"Thank you. I will be right back." The concierge stepped away to place the call to Brooklyn.

As Kali waited for the concierge to return, she couldn't help but overhear a woman next to her talking about something that sounded rather secret. "No, don't tell him I'm here, I want it to be a surprise. I would like my own room please. Thank you."

Kali turned her head, looked Shont'e up and down and snarled at her. Immediately, she wanted to slap her in her face for the pain she had caused Brooklyn, but she knew she had better keep her composure. She decided to play nice instead.

"Hi. You must be Shonte'." Kali reached her left hand out for a handshake.

Shonte' didn't reciprocate. She was used to groupies trying to be her friend to get to Brooklyn. "Do I know you?"

"No, but you will very soon." Kali had an underhanded look on her face, like she was already plotting and planning her revenge.

Shonte' noticed the ring on Kali's finger and her concerns vanished right away. "Oh my God! Can I see your hand again? That ring is amazing."

"Yeah my fiancé just proposed to me today," Kali said, in a crafty deceitful tone.

"Wow! That's amazing. He must be a great guy. You are a very lucky lady and his luck isn't so bad either. I mean you're beautiful. I'm sure he's a happy man. Just one word of advice." Shonte' grabbed

Kali's hand as if they had been friends for years and said, "No matter what just stay together. Work things out no matter how hard it gets.

Shonte' started getting teary eyed. Giving this stranger advice made her think about her own relationship.

"Um, yeah. Ok." Kali snatched her hand away from Shonte'. "Well I really must be going now, my fiancé is waiting for me. But we should have lunch together soon. I'm a reporter and I'm here do- ing a story on Brooklyn."

"That's a relief. For a second, I thought you were one of his groupies, but by the looks of that ring you've got your own man to deal with. What was your name again?"

"It's Kali. How about we have brunch together tomorrow?" Although Kali was enthused about the idea of having lunch with Shonte', she knew that if Brooklyn dragged his feet tonight she was gonna spill the beans.

"Sure, that sounds good. Do you have a card? I do some writing myself for a local column back home and it would be great to stay in touch. By the way, you are very beautiful. You should be doing some modeling."

"You know I'm fresh out of cards today. As soon as I get some more I will give you one. Enjoy the night and I will see you tomorrow."

"Sure thing, I can't wait," Shonte' said. Who knew making friends was so easy. Or was it. "Oh, and do me a favor, don't tell Brooklyn I'm here. I have a surprise for him."

"Don't you worry, I won't say a word. Nice meeting you."

*

Brooklyn was still in his room, frantically looking for flight info on Shonte'. Trying to find Shonte' was important but at that moment getting to his show, which he was already running late for, was more important. Trying to locate her was only making him later. He straightened up the room and left for his performance.

Shonte' was one floor up, directly above Brooklyn's room. She dressed herself in the same dress she wore the night they met at his show; the night he pulled her on stage and later fucked her in his backstage dressing room. She packed a pink nightie with matching pink slippers – identical to the ones she wore the first time they were together.

Shonte' was excited about seeing her lover and winning back his love, but she knew she had to do it the right way or risk losing his love forever. She thought about the advice Monique had given her and she knew if she didn't play her cards right, she would be pushing Brooklyn into the arms of another woman.

But that was the thing about Shonte' Smith, when it came to playing cards she was a spade champion and never reneged. Re-winning Brooklyn's love would be no different.

*

Chapter 10 Shonte'

Shonte' had a taxi follow Brooklyn's tour bus. Once he was on stage, she snuck into his dressing room, undressed and put on her pink nightie. She glanced around the room and she started to have a memory of the first time they made love backstage. She smiled as she tiptoed around the hollow, makeshift room.

"He's so spoiled," she said.

Brooklyn's favorite candy was gummi bears, but he hated the green ones – there was a bowl on the dressing room table with all of the green gummy bears taken out of the bunch.

"Celebrities," she mumbled

Shonte' paced back and forth awaiting her cue to be in a sexy ass-up position, just like she was the first time they had done this.

"Thank You Canada, I love you. Good night!" Brooklyn's signature sign-off line ran through the whole building.

Shonte' immediately ran to the couch and placed herself in that sexy ass-up position. Brooklyn walked in at exactly the right moment.

"Shonte'? What are you doing here?" He was startled and confused and the look on his face said it all. "Baby don't ask any questions. Just fuck me like you did the first time we were together. When we were brand new. Fuck me like you did before."

Brooklyn didn't know what to say or do. He was getting aroused but knew he needed to tell her what was going on. That thought lasted no longer than five seconds. He remembered their first time like it was yesterday. He remembered everything he had said and done to her that night. Shonte' was his dream girl and that moment with her that night was unforgettable for him. He recited every word exactly the same way he did the first time.

"I was hoping you'd be wearing that," he said. He grabbed her intensely and began to rub his hands down her spine. "Shonte', your body is so beautiful, soft and succulent. I want to taste every bit of you."

All of the thoughts of why he was with her started to formulate in his mind. "You like it when I fuck you like this huh? When I toss you around like an animal? Yeah you like when I fuck you from behind and hit hard from the back?"

"Yes, baby I like it from the back."

"You like it when I bite you?"

"Yes, baby bite my neck, I love it. Don't stop," she said. "Your muscles are so sexy baby," Shonte' groaned.

Brooklyn grabbed and pulled her hair from the back, then roughly pushed her down and forced himself inside her. "I know that's what you like, say my name."

"Brooklyn!"

"What's my name?"

"Brooklyn, baby. Brooklyn!"

"I'm about to put my whole body in you girl."

"I love it baby. I love your dick. You got the best in the world. I'm about to cum. Oh my God! I'm cumming!"

Brooklyn pumped hard once more and left his seeds inside of her.

"You ok?" he asked. He was still short of breath.

"Yeah I'm ok. Wow Brooklyn, we haven't done it like that in a long time."

"Well I'm glad I made you happy." Brooklyn stood up, put his shirt on and lit up a cigar. "Can you tell me again what you are doing here?" His face was puzzled.

"Well I thought I'd surprise you. Are you surprised?" Shonte' was starting to get a cold feeling from Brooklyn. "Come here. Why are you way over there? Are you still upset?"

"Shonte', upset isn't even the word... Try these on for size." Brooklyn started to count on his hand how many things he disliked. "Disappointed, ashamed, angry, heartbroken, hurt, violated – I mean, the list can go on and on and on. Matter a fact, you are ruining the moment. How about you just leave? I have an after party to get to."

"Wow, so you just gonna throw me out? Brooklyn, I said I'm sorry. What else do you want from me?"

"Right now, I want you to leave."

Shonte' began to cry. "I love you Brooklyn."

Brooklyn opened the door for her. Shonte' passed by him and asked, "So you not even gonna look at me?"

"Goodbye, Shonte'."

She stepped outside his dressing room and ran faster than she had ever run before. Outside, with tears falling from her face, she yelled for the nearest taxi.

Brooklyn was completely taken back by what just happened. He was pretending to be more upset with Shonte' than he really was.

Fuck, what am I going to do? He thought. *I got Shonte' here giving me the best pussy in the world and I got Kali badass loving the fucking ground I walk on. Fuck it, I'll deal with this shit tomorrow. I'm about to hit this after party.*

Brooklyn shut the door to his dressing room and made for the tour bus. He had no time for bullshit tonight. It was all about relief from here on out. He could fix this mess in the morning, right now it was party time.

*

Shonte' woke up with puffy eyes from all of the crying the night before. She went to look in the mirror. "Oh my God, I look like crap. I really don't even want to go, but it will be good for me to get out of this room."

Shonte' cleaned herself up, put on a little make up to disguise the bags under her eyes, and went downstairs to the restaurant to meet with Kali. They chose a table by the window. "It's so good to see you again, Shonte'. So, how was your night with Brooklyn? Did you surprise him?"

"Well I'd rather not discuss that with you. I don't have conversations about my love life with strangers, but thanks for asking." Shonte' gave her a side-eye look. "Listen Kali, if you're looking for some dirt on Brooklyn, you can get that on your own. I would never do anything to hurt him."

"Really?" Kali asked.

"Yes, really. I did a few Google searches on you and I couldn't find you anywhere under reporters. But, I did find a few albums and I know you're label mates with Brooklyn. So tell me what this is really about." Shonte' eyed Kali over her glass as she took a drink.

"Well..." Kali stopped mid-sentence as soon as she noticed Brooklyn looking in through the window.

"What the fuck are they doing together? This is some bullshit. Let me break this shit up right now," Brooklyn said, as he made his way to the door.

Brooklyn raced inside the restaurant. Shonte' stood up and kissed him on the lips. "Hey baby," he said. "I see you've met Kali."

"Yes sweetie, I did. She told me she was a reporter. I wonder why she would lie about that."

"Kali, don't you have a show to do?" Brooklyn asked. Brooklyn wasn't sure what Kali's response was going to be, but he was sure he would remain in control of the entire situation. If he was nervous he didn't show it.

"Actually, I don't, and I'd rather stay here and finish my conversation with Shonte'."

Brooklyn whistled for his security guards. They whisked in like a swat team. Brooklyn gave them a head nod in Kali's direction and they jumped into action "Ma'am I need you to come with me."

"Go with you? The fuck you mean go with you? I aint going no-muthafuckin-where."

The six-five, three hundred pound body guard grabbed Kali and picked her up and proceeded to carry her away.

"Get your hands off me, got damn it." Kali was kicking and screaming so hard she lost a shoe in the process. "Brooklyn! I'm going to kill you! After what we shared…"

The bodyguard quickly placed his hand over Kali's mouth to keep her from spilling the beans about their engagement.

"Babe, can you believe that?" Brooklyn asked.

"No baby I can't. She's acting more like a groupie than a singer. Why haven't I heard any of her albums?"

"She does mostly backup. Hey let's head up to your room and relax a little. I've been up all night with the boys."

"Ok baby. So, you forgive me?" Shonte' asked, a pleading look glazing her eyes.

"Let's talk about it upstairs." Brooklyn smacked Shonte' on the ass, watched her walk away with the switch of her hips and then followed right behind her.

When they arrived in Shonte's room, they kicked off their shoes and decided to relax from all the commotion. Shonte' lay on the bed and Brooklyn followed. Shonte' placed her hand on his chest and rubbed his bullet wounds. "Why don't you ever wanna talk about them?" she asked.

"There's not much to talk about. I got shot. What else is there to know?" Brooklyn moved her hand away from the wounds. "What are

159

you doing here anyway, for real? I told you I would get back to you, then you just pop up. That shit aint cool and ain't never been cool. Don't do that shit no more."

Shonte' sat up with her eyes big as day and a whimsical look on her face that was almost childlike. "Well I wanted to let you know that the police came to the house with a warrant. They were looking for you. They ransacked the house and left me with a huge mess to clean up. Do you care to explain why they keep coming back and why they are looking for you?"

"Look Shonte', like I told you before, the police will always be at our house. They will never find anything but they will always be looking. You knew about my lifestyle before you got involved with me. If it's too much for you to handle, let me know and I can always make it so you don't have to handle it." Brooklyn stood up as if he was going to leave the room and walk right out of Shonte's life forev- er.

"What? What are you talking about? Are you trying to break up with me?"

"Shonte', don't act like you don't know what's going on with us. You pop up here like nothing ever happened. You did what you did. I'm over it, but the fact still remains. You made a real decision without even discussing it with me. Period and point blank. The sooner you realize how fucked up that was, the sooner you will understand my response to you." Brooklyn's demeanor was calm but, on the in- side, he was furious, so much so that he had dented the table he was leaning on.

"Ok Brooklyn. I get it, I fucked up. But if we are going to be together then you are going to have to get over it. I mean…"

Brooklyn cut her off mid-sentence. "Get over it?" Brooklyn's lip was curled upwards in disbelief. "Get over it? You know what, I need some space. That's it. You can do whatever you want. If you wanna stay at this hotel or go home – whatever it is, I will pay for it. But if you do decide to stay here, I'm checking out."

"So last night meant nothing to you? I know you felt what I felt Brooklyn. You love me, why are you treating me like this?" Shonte' was distraught with emotions. She ran over to him, pleading for his love. "I'm sorry Brook… I made a mistake. I can't take it back, but please Brooklyn, let me try. I will do anything for you." Shonte' started to unbuckle his pants. "Let me show you. Let me please you."

"Really?" Brooklyn pulled away from her, buckled his pants and shook his head in disappointment. "Shonte', I thought you was better than that." He kissed her on her forehead. "Look, I got a show to do tonight so you can stay here. I will be checking out."

*

Chapter 11: The Break Up

The moment Brooklyn entered the hotel room was the same moment he knew something was up. It was strange for him to feel like this after a show. Usually he'd be on a major high and would want to spend the rest of his night drinking with his boys. Tonight though, he just wanted to know why the fuck his hotel room smelled like a mixture of spilled liquor and blood.

"Fuck," he exclaimed. "This shit is gonna cost a fortune to replace. Kali? Kali? Are you in here? Kali?" Brooklyn looked around and noticed there was broken glass everywhere, champagne bottles, wine glasses – it looked like Mike Tyson and Bruce Seldon had a fight right there in their room.

Brooklyn slowly gazed around the room and called out to Kali, but she still wasn't responding. He put his hand on the gun he was carrying in his waistband.

"Hello, is anybody in here?" Brooklyn crept around the hotel suite. Then he heard a crunch. He looked down and noticed he had stepped on a piece of broken glass. Brooklyn continued his search.

"Man, what the fuck happened in here?" Clothes were thrown everywhere, the T.V was busted and the sliding door to the balcony was wide open. Brooklyn crept through the room, trying to avoid the mess and made his way to the balcony. The cold Canada wind was blowing through the doors like a small hurricane. He stepped outside and still saw no sign of Kali. Or anyone for that matter. Still with one hand on his gun, he said, "Damn, where is she?"

Finally, it hit him. She's probably in the bathroom.

Tiptoeing back around through all the clutter, he noticed the bathroom light was on but the door was locked and closed.

"Kali are you in there?" He knocked hard, then harder. "Kali, if you are in there, open the door, the room looks like a tornado hit it. You wanna tell me what happened?"

Still there was no response. The room was so quiet you could hear a pin drop. "Kali come on, open the door. I know you're upset but this is ridiculous."

Then at that moment, Brooklyn looked down and saw something that would change his life forever.

"Is that blood?" Brooklyn threw his whole body at the door and it flew open. There she was, her lifeless body lying face down in a pool of her own blood. He felt for a pulse, but it was faint. He grabbed her hand and noticed the slits on both wrists. There was blood smeared across the floor; in the bathtub and on the mirror. This was even too much for Brooklyn to handle.

"I've seen a lot of shit but I ain't never seen no shit like this."

He yelled for help but no one heard him. It was like time was frozen and he could see the angels coming for Kali. Speckles of light entered the room. He tried to console her but he was fearing the worst. "It's ok baby…" A tear fell from his eye. "Kali please… Please, Kali, please wake up."

He grabbed a couple of towels and pressed one onto each wrist to stop the bleeding. It was the most powerless act the world had ever seen. Brooklyn realized that heaven would be taking another angel tonight, but not just any angel. Tonight, it was his angel. Tonight, it was Kali.

His bodyguard finally arrived and saw Brooklyn trying to keep Kali alive. "Man, what the fuck happened?"

There was blood everywhere. It was on the beautiful marble floors and on the white walls. Even the ceiling was coated in the red remnants of the liquid that once filled her veins. Kali had been able to write out a message on the wall in red writing before she passed out.

Love Hurts

Brooklyn and his bodyguard managed to grab Kali and take her out of the back exit of the hotel. Brooklyn already knew there were no cameras that covered the rear exit, and that's exactly why they left through it.

The car vibrated beneath them as the Bentley roared out of the parking lot. Brooklyn sat in the backseat and held Kali. He kept applying pressure to her wounds and assured her she would be ok. Though that was more to comfort himself than anything else, because there's no way on earth she could hear him in her state.

He watched as blood continued to ooze from her wounds like an eruption from a volcano. "Man, Imma need you to get us there or she's gonna die. Just get us there man."

The rubber screeched against the pavement as the Bentley came to an abrupt halt right outside the emergency door. Before Big Psyche could even turn off the engine, Brooklyn had already jumped from the backseat and dragged Kali through the automatic doors. "Somebody help me! Please help me."

The doctors, nurses and patients all looked at him like they were afraid to budge. Brooklyn was covered in Kali's blood and he looked like a crazy man on a murdering spree.

"Sir, I can help," a doctor replied. He gathered a crew to assist him, they lay her on the gurney and whisked her into the operating room.

"Please doctor, please save her." Brooklyn was bawling and overwhelmed with the fear of losing Kali.

As the doctors and nurses swarmed around Kali, one important-looking guy with an extra white lab coat and a golden pin attached to the pocket approached Brooklyn. "Sir, what happened to her? Her wounds are vicious."

Brooklyn couldn't even begin to form a response. The whirlwind that was swarming in his mind wouldn't even allow a complete sentence to form. All he could do was stand and stare in the direction they had taken Kali.

*

Chapter 12: Deranged

Brooklyn and his bodyguard took a seat in the waiting room. He was still dazed and confused about what just occurred and he had to say it out loud.

"Psyche can you believe this shit? No really? Can you believe what just happened?" Brooklyn inching closer to Psyche and whispered. "Man, she just tried to fucking kill herself in my hotel room. Man, what the fuck? There is so much to deal with." Brooklyn in- haled and put both hands on his head, then slowly exhaled.

"Just calm down man, ain't no use in getting all worked up," Psyche said.

"Man, the police are gonna get involved. I already got cases back in New York that I'm fighting them on. Man, I really can't believe this shit just happened. Bro I'm so fucked up, I don't know whether to cry for Kali or go on the run. The first person the police is gone come looking for is me. Fuck man!"

"Bro, just calm down. You know I got you and don't worry about the police. This is Canada, things operate differently out here. You ain't gotta worry about that. I will handle that part. You just get your- self together so you can be alright when she wakes up."

"Yeah, I guess you're right. Thanks man," Brooklyn said.

While they were waiting, they noticed a few people whispering and pointing over at them. "Oh fuck, here we go with this shit," Brooklyn grumbled.

"Hey you're M.C. Brooklyn, aren't you? Hey, I don't believe it."

Cameras started flashing and people started taking pictures. Brooklyn's bodyguard immediately placed a call for backup, and re-quested a private waiting room.

*

Twenty minutes later, Brooklyn sat in one of the dark empty hospital rooms awaiting the doctor's news about Kali. The room was cold, dark and empty – a lot like how he was feeling. As his mind started to wonder if Kali was going to make it or not, the doctor walked in and opened his folder.

"Ok well, she's alive, but she's still unconscious. She lost a huge amount of blood and slipped into a coma. If you guys hadn't gotten here when you did she probably wouldn't have made it. If you'd like to see her you can come with me. Just remember, she's unresponsive."

Brooklyn and the doctor started their way down the long corridor, the doctor continued to explain Kali's state while they were walking.

"I think she will pull through but we won't know the damage that's caused until she's alert. Oh, and don't be startled by the bandages, it looks a lot worse than it really is."

Brooklyn didn't know if the doctor was just saying this as a coping mechanism for him or not, but he knew Kali was in pretty bad shape and prepared himself for the worst. He took a deep breath in and exhaled and mentally coaxed himself through what he was about to see.

The door crept open slowly. Brooklyn could hear all the beep- ing machines before he could see them. Beep. Beep. Beep. He felt like the machines were taunting him.

"Ok I will leave you two alone," the doctor said. "If you need anything just let me know."

Brooklyn just stood there in disbelief; once again, his heart was broken, and he had no idea how to put it back together. Kali just lay there helpless with tubes running through every hole in her body and machines breathing for her.

"Look at this shit, all these tubes going in and out of your body. Why did you do this Kali? Why? Huh?" His voice crackled like he wanted to cry, but he held back the tears.

Brooklyn's bodyguard stepped in to check on him. "Hey man, you alright?"

"Yeah I'm good bro. I just need a few more minutes alone with her."

"Sure, I'll wait outside."

Brooklyn sat on the side of the bed and said to Kali, "I am so sorry I hurt you baby, I never meant for any of this to happen. I love you and I just need you to come back to me." A tear fell from his eye and he softly kissed her forehead and exited the room.

"You good bro?" Psyche asked.

"Yeah, I'm as good as good gone get. Let's bounce."

They stopped at the nurse's station and left a one-hundred dollar tip. As he handed the cash over, Brooklyn said, "Hey, here's my number. Can you call me and let me know if she wakes up?"

"Of course, I can. Thanks," the nurse replied.

He heard it before he saw it, but by the time he could respond it was already too late. The mob poured through the revolving doors like Hurricane Katrina. Luckily for him, Psyche was on his toes, and he managed to drag Brooklyn back into the corridor just in the nick of time.

They bolted back along the corridor they'd just walked down and managed to duck out the side of the building, through an unmonitored emergency exit. They hopped in the black Bentley that pulled up right as they broke out into the open air and gunned it out of the hospital parking lot.

Brooklyn was quiet the entire ride back to the hotel.

He thought about Shonte' Kali and the role he played in all of it. It was like no matter how much money he had; nothing could solve the problems he had created for himself. Initially, he thought nothing was wrong with what he was doing. He had put it in his mind that he was actually doing both Shonte' and Kali a favor by being with them, but now he was starting to realize that it had gotten out of hand and he needed to put an end to the madness.

His life was chaotic, and he finally had to admit to himself that he was in love with two women at the same time. He didn't want to talk about it, so he sent Shonte' a text instead.

Hey I need you to pack your bags and go back to New York. I don't have time to explain and go into detail about my decision. I will send you a plane ticket and get you a car. There's a lot going on with me right now. I just need some time to clear my mind and that needs to be without you. Your ticket and flight info will be arriving via email shortly. Peace and I will see you soon.

Brooklyn scanned the contents of his text one last time, hit send, and rested his head against the cool leather of the seat. It stayed there all the way back to the hotel.

*

Chapter 13: Reality Bites

Brooklyn stayed in Canada and continued his shows. A few days went by and Kali was still in a coma. He had flowers sent, cards and candy. He even stopped by a few times, but seeing her in that condition bothered him to a degree he couldn't handle. So, the visits became less and less frequent.

Kali didn't have any family, so it was all left to Brooklyn. He called the hospital hourly, but her condition was always the same. Brooklyn wasn't religious but he found himself talking to God.

Father, if you exist, I ask you to do me a solid. Please bring her back. Please.

Minutes went by like hours for Brooklyn. Kali still in her coma, and Shonte' still in New York.

Brooklyn contacted her only to send money and cover the bills. He found no reason to contact her otherwise. Brooklyn was a man of his word and like his daddy used to say, a man should always follow a code that he will live and die by. It hadn't made a lot of sense to

Brooklyn growing up, but now it made all the sense in the world, and Brooklyn intended to abide by the code.

*

Chapter 14: New York, New York

Shonte' continued her writing and dedicated herself to her craft. She even got a job working at a well-known hip hop magazine. She did everything she could to keep her mind off Brooklyn, but his celebrity status always kept him relevant. She even found out what had happened with Kali from the celebrity gossip channel.

There was footage of Brooklyn exiting the hospital. Shonte' couldn't understand why Brooklyn was so interested in Kali. Shonte' couldn't make sense of it all, and neither did she want to. She decided to block him out of her mind entirely and honor his request to be left alone.

*

Chapter 15: The Awakening

Watching the world pass by through the back seat of his Bentley had become procedural for Brooklyn, or at least that's how it seemed. But today was a little different. Today he managed to crack a smile.

He had gotten the call when he was in the middle of lifting weights. The nurse called and told him that it's a miracle, but Kali is awake and fully responsive. It was totally unexpected to have her back to consciousness at all, but factor in the short amount of time it had taken, this was nothing short of a miracle.

As the Bentley pulled up to the hospital Brooklyn told the driver to let him out at the front door. He entered the double doors with memories of his last visit. He cracked a smile and walked right over to the nurse's station.

"I'm here to see Kali Graham."

"Oh yes sir, she's in room three, go right ahead."

When he entered the room, Kali was awake and looking refreshed. He was so happy to see her eyes open.

Brooklyn stepped to his left to face the man with the lab coat and clipboard, more because he looked important than anything else. "So, is she ok doc? As in, is she ok-ok?"

"She has some memory loss. She doesn't seem to know why she's here, but you were the first person she asked for when she woke. She's been telling all the nurses that she's getting married."

"That's great. Thanks doc."

Brooklyn sat next to Kali on the edge of the bed. "How are you, have they been taking care of you here?"

"Yes, I guess so. At least from what I can remember."

"Kali you scared the fuck out of me. I thought you were going to die. You have no idea what you have put me through these past few days."

"Oh, I'm sorry, honey. I didn't mean to upset you." She softly rubbed Brooklyn on his forearm. "I hate hospitals, and I would like to get out of here. Can you take me home, please, babe?"

"Let me check with the doctor."

Brooklyn went to the nurse's station and got the approval to take Kali home. Brooklyn packed up Kali's things and wheeled her out of the hospital. They weren't going home, they were going someplace else. Someplace special. Someplace far away from the memory of razor blades and bloodied hotel rooms.

*

When they arrived, Kali felt like a little girl again. Her father always took care of her when she was sick, and Brooklyn reminded her of that.

"I love it, Brooklyn. I think this will really help with my recovery." Her eyes were as bright as the sun, and it felt like Brooklyn had fallen for her all over again.

Brooklyn wheeled her into the log cabin and swiftly tidied the home for her.

"Brooklyn, stop. There are some things I can do for myself, you know. You don't have to do everything."

Brooklyn picked her up from the wheelchair and lay her in the bed. "Here is a bell if you need me, just ring it. I will be in the next room."

"Wait. Before you go, tell me why I have these scars on my wrists?"

Brooklyn walked over to her intensely, looked into her eyes, and said, "Let's talk about that later, okay?"

Brooklyn knew Kali was feeling better and decided to get to New York to have a conversation with Shonte', but he had to break the news to Kali.

"Look, I'm not about to play games with you or her. I love both of you, and I'm not going to choose. I will say this: my life is complicated. I have never been a simple kind of guy, so simple shit just doesn't work for me." Brooklyn stood up as if he were a boss conducting a meeting with his employees.

"Complicated? What the fuck you mean complicated? Life is complicated, Brooklyn; nothing is ever simple. Do you care to explain this to me further?"

Brooklyn walked over towards the window, gazed out of it and replied, "Shonte' understands my life and has never had a problem with it. I don't know if you are ready for all of that."

"But I thought we were getting married."

"Kali, I thought so too. But not right now. I have a few things to handle, but I love you, and I will be back."

Brooklyn walked right out of the cabin doors, and Kali felt like he was walking right out of her life. She watched teary-eyed as the Range Rover drove off in the snow.

Brooklyn wasn't alone in this game of tales and lies. Kali was holding her own secret.

She remembered everything about the night she tried to commit suicide, and she wasn't the least bit ready for Brooklyn to leave her side. Kali knew once he left, she could lose him forever. She also knew Brooklyn loved Shonte', but she was not about to share him.

Kali slid from the bed and trudged over to her suitcase. She unzipped it and fumbled around for a few moments. The small wooden case she was looking for couldn't be left in plain sight. When she found it, she hugged the case close to her chest. It was something she had known would come in useful one day.

She got dressed, headed outside, started up her car, and set out to pay a surprise visit to Brooklyn and Shonte'.

*

Chapter 16: The Prophecy Continued

"Oh my God Brooklyn. Wake up!" Shonte' said in a panic as she nudged Brooklyn.

He woke up rubbing his eyes. "What Shonte'?"

They were laying in their king-size bed. Brooklyn turned on the light, and to his surprise Kali was standing over the both of them with a nine-millimeter gun pointed directly at them. Brooklyn was still in disbelief. He continued rubbing his eyes, thinking maybe if he rubbed them hard enough she would go away.

"Kali? What the fuck are you doing?"

Kali just stood there with tears running down her face. "You said we were gonna get married Brooklyn." Her voice was teary. "You said you were gonna marry me."

"Kali, please put the gun down. We can talk about this. Kali, I still love you."

"What?" Shonte' exclaimed.

"Bitch you shut the fuck up," Kali screamed. "Just shut up. This is all your fault. You broke his heart, and he came to me. To me," she yelled. "I have loved him for so long. You had him and treated him like shit. You don't deserve him. You deserve to die…" Kali cocked back the gun. "Die, bitch! Die!"

Kali was firing so many shots that it started to sound like a firing range. She fired every round in the clip and kept squeezing the trigger long after it released nothing more than the clicking sound of an empty magazine.

"No… No… No…"

Brooklyn walked in and shook Shonte' as she rolled around and yelled in her sleep. "Wake up, Shonte', wake up."

"Oh my God! Brooklyn, I just had the worst dream." She hugged him as he sat on the edge of their bed. Her body trembled so much that she almost fell out of Brooklyn's arms.

"Are you ok?" he asked. Brooklyn kissed her forehead and held her tighter "You're shaking really bad. What's wrong?"

"Brooklyn, I dreamed that Kali came here, and she tried to kill us." Brooklyn released her from his grip, stood up and said,

"Shonte', I have told you over and over again to chill out with those dreams, girl. Kali don't even know where we stay at. You been watching too much TV."

"Brooklyn, I know there's more to that story about you and her, but I will let you have that. I don't want to know about it. I am just glad you're home. But we need to leave here tonight. We can't stay."

"Shonte' I just got home. I'm tired. I just wanna lay here next to you and relax. I also want to tell you I'm sorry for staying away so long. That was dumb, and regardless of the reason, I shouldn't have had you hanging on like that."

"Brooklyn, I deserved it. I am so sorry I hurt you. That was never what I intended."

"Ok. I understand. We don't have to talk about it anymore. I'm home and I'm staying home. I miss you. You haven't been fucking nobody else, have you?"

"No baby, this pussy is all yours."

"Well, I guess we will see right now, won't we?" Brooklyn got undressed and lay down in the bed next to Shonte'.

She climbed on top of him and placed his erect penis inside of her. She rode him hard and fast. "Tell me you love me Brooklyn."

"I love you baby."

"Say it again."

"I love you baby." Brooklyn rubbed her nice round breasts.

Shonte' was enjoying every moment of Brooklyn but she was still distracted by her dream. She continued to give him the ride of his life. "Is that how you like it baby? You miss me? You miss this bomb-ass pussy don't you?"

"Yeah, I miss this shit right here"

Shonte' gazed around the room but didn't stop her hips from circling to Brooklyn's body. Something just didn't feel right. "Baby I think we need to go," Shonte' said, with Brooklyn still inside her.

"Baby I'm not going nowhere, but Imma be coming if you keep riding my dick like that. Damn girl, if I knew you was gone be fucking me like this I would've came home a long time ago."

"Brooklyn, feel my heartbeat." He put his hand on her left breast. "You feel that. My heartbeat's the same as yours."

"Wait, what was that?" Brooklyn asked.

"What was that baby? I didn't hear anything."

"It sounded like it was coming from outside."

"You feel that baby? Our souls are connecting, and we are one. It's like my soul was sad, lonely, and depressed until yours danced its way into mine, and now all I can feel is heaven running through my entire being." Shonte' was riding him like she had never done before.

"Damn, that feels good, baby." Brooklyn allowed her to take control of his body. He gazed at her in amazement and enjoyment. Watching her in action was all he needed.

"Yeah. Yeah, I feel it." Shonte' was still on top and she wasn't ready to release her power. She rocked with him up and down back and forth. Stroking his dick like a guitar strum.

"Wait babe, I think I did hear something this time. For real," Shonte' said.

"No, don't move. Our spirits are connecting. My body is tingling, and I feel like I am on the best rollercoaster of my life. You're about to make me come," Brooklyn said. He stared at her as the intense feeling crept closer and closer. She had tears in her eyes, and her emotions took over. Shonte, are you crying? "

"Yes."

"What's wrong? You wanna stop?"

"No baby. I love it. Don't stop."

Brooklyn continued to let Shonte' take control over his body. Each time she rolled her hips towards him he caught her like they were playing a sport. Shonte' rode him in circles, frontwards and backwards until he screamed, "Fuck! Shonte', I love you."

Shonte' lay on top of him, kissed his chest and climbed off of him. She lay next to him and dozed off.

*

Chapter 17: Kali's Revenge

Kali was there watching the both of them through their bedroom door. "This bitch thinks she's just gonna fuck my man and get away with it? Well, she's got another thing coming. I bet you didn't see me coming, did you miss Shonte'?"

Kali tightened the grip on her handgun and slowly pushed the door open further to get a better view, but there was a shallow creek.

"What was that?" Shonte' asked.

"What was what? I'm sure it was nothing. Ain't nobody tryna run up in here. Baby, I'm M.C. Brooklyn. Now go back to sleep."

"I guess you're right. Aint nobody tryna see the Brook," she said sarcastically. Shonte' leaned in closer to him and hugged him from behind. She closed her eyes and dozed back off to sleep.

Kali crept around in their bedroom, first noticing the pictures on Brooklyn and Shonte's dresser.

"Aw, what a cute couple, too bad it won't last. He's mine bitch." Kali removed the picture from its frame, balled it up, and tossed it aside. All without making a peep. She dragged her index finer along the dresser, tracing its shape as if it were giving her ideas for her next move. Next, she was onto Shonte's walk-in closet.

"Oh, you spoiled-ass little bitch. Versace, Donna Karen, Chanel, Gucci. Got damn, you sure got a lot of shit for a bitch that only works part-time for a low-budget city paper." She inhaled the clothing with a smile as if, for one moment, she was in Shonte's place – wearing her clothes, fucking Brooklyn, and escorting him on red carpet-events.

She dragged the gun across Shonte's magnificent gowns. "Now this is how a bitch should live." Kali sat down at the vanity counter where Shonte's makeup and wigs lay. "So, Brooklyn, this is what you like. Ok." Kali picked up a red Mac lipstick that was lying on the counter and smeared it across her face. She rubbed the lipstick so hard and long that it broke in the process.

"So, this is what you want huh?" she said, talking to herself in the mirror. Kali powdered her face with all of Shonte's makeup, put on one of her wigs, and even sprayed some of Shonte's perfume on her neck and ears.

"How beautiful," she said as she glared at the person before her. "Oh, and one last thing. I can't forget the most important thing of all. My red ballroom gown. He is going to love this." Kali sat the gun down on the chase and slipped into one of Shonte's red carpet gowns she had worn to an awards ceremony with Brooklyn.

Kali took one last look in the full-sized mirror in front of her and said, "Now that's better, fucking exquisite. There's no way he will say no now."

She picked up the gun and softly crept back into the bedroom where Shonte' and Brooklyn lay sound asleep. She watched them temporarily as if she was studying their sleeping habits. With her head tilted to one side, she said softly, "Aw how beautiful, just fucking beautiful."

She sadistically admired them while they slept. Then out of nowhere Kali snapped, like a light had flicked on in her hand. She grabbed Shonte' by her hair and dragged her out the bed.

"Wake the fuck up, bitch."

"What the fuck are you doing? Let me go." Shonte' was trying to remove Kali's extraordinary grip from her head.

"Bitch, you move one more time and I will put a bullet in your fucking face. You hear me?"

Shonte' continued to struggle.

"What the fuck is going on?" Brooklyn yelled "Kali?" He reached to turn on the lamp on the side of the bed.

"Don't you fucking move Brooklyn, I will shoot this bitch," Kali said with an angry and tear-filled voice. "Brooklyn, don't try me. I will do it."

"Ok Kali. What the fuck? Why are you wearing Shonte's clothes? How long have you been here? Ok, you are taking this way too far. Put the fucking gun down Kali."

"I'm not putting shit down until you explain to me why you left me, Brooklyn!" A tear dropped from her eye. Kali was so amped up on adrenaline that she practically foamed at the mouth.

"Have you told her yet?" Kali asked. "I said, have you told her yet?" she yelled, clenching her hand to Shonte's ponytail.

"Kali, I told you to let me handle it," Brooklyn said.

"Told her what?" Shonte' asked while still trying to loosen Kali's kung-fu grip. "What is she talking about, Brooklyn?" Shonte' asked in a demanding tone.

"Oh ok... I see you haven't told her. You see this fucking ring on my finger that you admired so much? Yeah bitch, take a long hard look at it. We're getting married, and as soon as I am done with you, we will have the wedding of my dreams, and it will be me sleeping peacefully beside him, not you."

"Brooklyn, is she serious?" Shonte' could feel her heart breaking all over again.

"Damn right I'm serious."

"Ouch bitch, fucking let me go," Shonte' said.

"Oh, you haven't seen nothing yet. You haven't even begun to experience pain."

During Kali's tangent Brooklyn managed to reach in the drawer and pull out his piece. He slipped in underneath the covers with him.

"Yeah, Shonte', it's all true. I just came home to get some of that good good one last time. It's all true. Kali and I are getting married and I am going to be with her forever."

"What? What are you talking about?" Shonte' replied. She was trying to remember how it all went down in her dream, but her emotions got the best of her, and she couldn't even focus straight.

Her mind was racing a million miles a minute. Normally, handling this type of situation would be easy for her, but her love for Brooklyn overpowered her mentally.

"Don't you fucking move," Kali said, waving the gun back and forth between Shonte' and Brooklyn.

"Babe, I'm just going to come over to you so I can kiss you slowly. You miss me? Is it ok if I come near you?"

"Ok, but no funny business, or she gets it right in the face. I mean it, Brooklyn, don't play with me"

Brooklyn stood up and calmly made his way towards Kali and Shonte'. With his hands raised in the air, he said, "Baby, you know you are the love of my life, and I would never do anything to hurt you." He inched closer to her. "You know that, right?" Brooklyn was now close enough to touch her. He put both of his hands on her head and kissed her lips.

Kali's grip loosened on Shonte' and she managed to get away from Kali's demented control and crawled over towards her side of the bed.

"See what you made me do, Brooklyn; why did you make me do this? It would have been so much easier if you had kept your word." Kali was still holding the gun loosely in her hand.

"I know, baby, and I was wrong for that. Come here and sit down on the bed with me. Relax, and let Daddy take care of you. Ok?"

Kali complied. They walked over to the bed.

"Yeah, just relax." Brooklyn gently sat Kali down on the bed and knelt down beside her.

"So... we can still be together, right? Get married, have a house with a white picket fence and kids, right?"

"Of course, baby. Why not?" Brooklyn was trying to reach for the gun hidden behind him, tucked into his boxer waistband, but he was too slow.

Shonte' reached into her nightstand drawer pulled out a .38 and took aim. "Shit Brooklyn, move." Her palms were sweaty, and her heart pounded like a bass drum.

"Why don't you love me, Brook? Why?" Kali asked

"This is why, bitch." Shonte' rose up from behind them, but Kali was quick. Quicker than either of them expected.

Both guns go off simultaneously, and there is a thud.

To be continued…

*

Note from Miss T. Lane

Hope you enjoyed it. See what happens next in Steamy Dreams 3. God Bless Kings and Queens, and thank you for allowing me into your hearts and your minds. Until next time. Have a Steamy Dream on me!

To be Continued…

Thank You for Reading!

If you enjoyed *Steamy Dreams 2: Kali's Revenge*, I would truly appreciate it if you left a review.

Reviews help independent authors like me reach more readers and continue telling stories that matter.

Leave your thoughts on Amazon:

www.amazon.com/author/missteelane

Tag us on social media with your favorite quote or scene:

IG: @moores.publishing | #SteamyDreamsSeries

With love and drama,

Ms. T. Lane

About the Author

Ms. T. Lane is a bestselling author, publisher, and unapologetic voice in urban romance and women's empowerment. Hailing from Compton, California, she brings a bold, streetwise perspective to every story she writes—blending raw emotion, real-life struggles, and irresistible drama.

She is the author of the steamy and addictive *Steamy Dreams* series and the transformative self-help guide *Sis, Shut Up and Listen*. As the founder of Moore's Publishing House, Ms. T. Lane helps aspiring authors publish powerful stories while keeping full control of their creative rights and royalties.

When she's not writing or coaching, she's mentoring youth, building generational wealth, or cheering on her two children—her son, a rising basketball player, and her daughter, an aspiring sports journalist.

Follow her journey and publishing empire on Instagram: @moores.publishing

BOOKS IN THIS SERIES

Steamy Dreams (Book 1 of the Steamy Dreams Series)

Shonté Smith appears to have it all—career success, a stable marriage, and a picture-perfect life. But when the dreams start… everything changes. Vivid, erotic, and unsettling, her nighttime fantasies star two very real men from her past: Ronny, her college sweetheart turned NFL superstar, and Brooklyn, a magnetic rapper from her hometown with unfinished business between them.

As the line between dream and desire begins to blur, Shonté finds herself entangled in a steamy, emotional whirlwind that threatens to unravel the carefully curated life she's built. What starts as fantasy quickly spirals into temptation—and then reality.

Will Shonté risk it all for the thrill of what could have been, or fight to hold on to the life she's worked so hard to build?

Steamy Dreams is the first installment in a bold, addictive urban romance series that explores the complexity of love, loyalty, and lust. If you enjoy high heat, high stakes, and emotionally charged storytelling, this is the series for you.